THE SECRET LIFE OF
JENNY LIU

Jean Ramsden

Jabber & Jam Books
Davidson, North Carolina

Jean Ramsden/Jabber & Jam Books
99 Jackson Street, Unit #2216
Davidson, North Carolina 28036

Publisher's Note: This is a work of fiction. Names, characters, places, and incidents are a product of the author's imagination. Locales and public names are sometimes used for atmospheric purposes. Any resemblance to actual people, living or dead, or to businesses, companies, events, institutions, or locales is completely coincidental.

Book Layout ©2013 BookDesignTemplates.com

Ordering Information:
Quantity sales. Special discounts are available on quantity purchases by corporations, associations, and others. For details, contact the "Special Sales Department" at the address above.

The Secret Life of Jenny Liu/ Jean Ramsden. -- 1st ed.
ISBN 978-0-9913524-0-1

To J.R., H.R. and W.F.

The person who removes a mountain begins by carrying away small stones.

—*Chinese Proverb*

Monday, February 1: The Worst Eight Minutes Ever

The door banged shut and Jenny Liu found herself, once again, stuck in the waiting area of the principal's office without an escape plan. Her armpits began to leak rivers, rivers that felt like giant oceans; giant, smelly oceans. Jenny sighed, not because she had already managed to ruin her brand-new shirt, but because she knew the day was only going to get worse, much worse. Sweat stains were the least of her problems.

When Principal Brimstone waddled out of his office, the only thing Jenny noticed was his upside-down head. The top was completely bald but hair sprouted like weeds from his ears. His bushy moustache was filled with crumbs. Principal Brimstone reminded Jenny of a walrus she had once watched sunbathe on a rock at Sea World—short and fat, bald yet hairy, with fish pieces scattered all over his whiskers. California seemed like such a long time ago. But when she thought about it, Jenny realized that the Sea World trip had only been a month earlier, right before her parents dropped the bomb that they would be moving again.

"Well, welcome to Haverswell Elementary School, Jenny! My name is Principal Brimstone. I'm sure you're going to have a swell time here!"

Principal Brimstone laughed, his huge smile setting off an avalanche of crumbs down the front of his shirt. A big piece of biscuit stuck to Jenny's hand and she stood paralyzed with embarrassment. Pretending to smooth her shirt, Jenny tried to flick the crumb onto the floor. Instead, it landed smack in the middle of a poster that read, "Fly High, Haverswell Hawks!" Principal Brimstone was laughing too hard to notice. Jenny nervously played with her long, dark hair and started counting down on the wall clock. The First Day Introduction, otherwise known as The Worst Eight Minutes Ever, had officially begun.

"Haverswell. Have-A-Swell," Principal Brimstone laughed. "Get it, Short Stack?" Jenny's eyes shifted toward the floor and for the first time since they had met, Principal Brimstone was quiet. When she was first learning how to speak English and she didn't understand something, people often stared at her as if she was a teeny, tiny baby, but never with as much sympathy as Principal Brimstone did now. He was even pouting his lip.

"HAVERSWELL. HAVE. A. SWELL," he repeated. Louder did not help. It never did. Principal Brimstone sounded like an alien to Jenny, an alien trying to make a joke. Jenny wished she could melt into the carpet.

"Oh, bless your heart," Principal Brimstone said, gently patting her on the arm. "I reckon our southern accents will take some gettin' used to, just like the biscuits." He brushed some crumbs off his shirt and Jenny prayed that she wouldn't be hit again. "Come on, sugar, let's go meet your new teacher and your new class," he said. Just before the door shut behind them, Jenny looked back at the clock. One minute down. Seven to go.

Principal Brimstone and Jenny walked in silence through hallways whose unfamiliar twists and turns, doors with strange names and colorful artwork made her dizzy. She imagined herself as Alice falling down the rabbit hole with no idea where she was going or when she would reach the end. Then she imagined her mother as the White Rabbit reminding her over and over that meeting a new class was just part of moving and not, as Jenny believed, a horror story waiting to happen.

Moving five times in eleven years meant that Jenny had spent almost half her life starting over or as she considered it, half her life falling down the rabbit hole. Her father's work transferred him every two years and although she acted surprised, Jenny always knew when they were moving because it was the only occasion besides her birthday that she ever got to go a fancy Chinese restaurant. It was impossible for Jenny to throw a temper tantrum if she was dressed in her best silk dress and surrounded by not only a room full of strangers, but waiters who delivered a new course every five minutes.

As Principal Brimstone led her down yet another hallway, Jenny held out a small amount of hope that this first day would be different. Instead of being crushed by embarrassment, maybe she could sneak into an empty chair without being noticed. But Jenny had started a new school four times before, and sneaking and disappearing wasn't the way being the new kid worked. Being new meant being noticed, feeling weird and worst of all, being forced to speak in front of a room full of strangers. The only difference, thought Jenny, was that this first day would happen in Haverswell, South Carolina, a place she had never set foot in until a few weeks ago.

When they arrived at room 147, Principal Brimstone walked Jenny through the door. A teacher with hot pink lipstick and blonde pig tails skipped toward them. "Well, aren't you a sight for sore eyes, Miss Candy!" Principal Brimstone said. Automatically, Jenny translated the word "candy" into Chinese and smiled. Her new teacher, who wore a rainbow tutu, did indeed look like a piece of candy. Cotton candy.

Ms. Candy wrapped her arms around Jenny, who in return, stood as stiff as a mannequin. Jenny wondered how she could explain that people rarely hugged in the Chinese culture—not parents and their children, not teachers and their students, not friends and especially, not in public. Jenny stepped away from Ms. Candy to show her respect, but instead her new teacher looked upset that she hadn't hugged her back.

Oblivious of Jenny's discomfort, Principal Brimstone said, "Class, this here is Jenny Liu." When twenty-four pairs of eyes stared back at her, Jenny started to sweat again, her face burning up like a plate of spicy dan dan noodles. "She came all the way from California to be with your class until the end of the year," he continued. "Isn't that somethin'?"

The answer came in the form of a gigantic burp followed by the class' laughter. From the front a proper-looking girl with a perfectly lip-glossed smile shouted, "That's disgusting, Aidan!" to a chubby boy with shaggy hair in the back row. Aidan burped even louder. Jenny was shocked by all the noise. In her other schools, students talked only when the teacher called on them. But, Jenny was also thankful. She had already made it halfway. Four minutes left to go.

"Well, I'm sure y'all will have a swell time together!" Principal Brimstone laughed as he turned to leave. Jenny looked around for clues about the joke, but the class was busy fidgeting with their pencils or slumped over their desks, heads buried like hermit crabs inside their arms. Ms. Candy twirled her hair.

Jenny was wondering if maybe she wasn't the only one who didn't understand Principal Brimstone when the girl from the front row sang out, "We always have a swell day at Haverswell Elementary School, Principal Brimstone!"

As he walked out the door, Principal Brimstone gave her a thumbs-up. She seemed pleased with herself until Aidan began teasing, "Nadia's a teacher's pet! Nadia's a teacher's pet!" Nadia glared toward the back row. Aidan let out an even louder burp and Nadia pointed her nose into the air. Aidan imitated her and Nadia stuck out her tongue at him. Jenny thought that more opposite people didn't exist.

In a room full of burping, laughter and name-calling, for the first time ever in the history of The First Day Introduction, Jenny actually forgot that she was in front of the class until Ms. Candy hugged her again and said, "We're so happy that you're here, Jenny!" While her head was stretched awkwardly over Ms. Candy's shoulder, Jenny noticed the clock and was thankful for the third time that day. Eight minutes had already passed. Jenny sat down and felt herself disappear into the only empty desk.

"And hot dog, am I happy it's February!" said Ms. Candy, clapping her hands together. "The next two weeks are full of fun!" But as soon as Ms. Candy wrote "FUN#1: SPELLING BEE" on the chalkboard, the class acted just the opposite of fun, groaning and falling against the back of their chairs as if she had just announced that spinach would be on the lunch menu every day. Only one person seemed excited—Nadia.

"Why even bother studying?" moaned Aidan as Ms. Candy passed out the spelling word lists. "Nadia wins every year!"

"Who knows," said Ms. Candy as she grinned at Jenny, "this year may be different." Jenny squirmed at the attention, especially when Nadia made a point of scowling at her. "ALL the fifth graders will practice the word lists and ALL the fifth graders will participate in the class spelling bee. The fifth-grade winner will receive movie tickets and get a chance to compete in the school-wide bee."

The girl sitting next to Jenny leaned toward her desk and said, "You're probably, like, so good at like, spelling. I pretty much, like, stink." The girl pointed to "LILLY" on the back of her shiny soccer shirt and said, "Hi, I'm Lilly, World's Best Goal-Scorer." Then, looking at her word list she sighed and said, "World's Worst Speller." Jenny desperately wanted to tell Lilly the truth, which was that she was probably even worse at spelling and that being Chinese didn't necessarily mean you were smart. Instead, Jenny smiled politely.

Although Jenny had moved a lot, she had always lived in big cities in California and she had always attended Chinese-American schools. Many of her classes were taught in Chinese and she was one of a hundred kids with an Asian last name. Exactly three other Asian kids went to Haverswell Elementary. Jenny would be the only fifth grader. In an attempt to make her feel like less of an outcast, Jenny's mother had pointed out the Park twins when they were at the piano studio to sign up for lessons. But, the Park twins were Korean, in first grade and boys. Jenny didn't think that they had anything whatsoever in common.

And then there was Eddie Wang, who she had met at church. Eddie was just a year older, but he was still a boy. Plus, he was only half-Chinese. Jenny knew lots of half-Chinese kids who actually looked Asian, but Eddie was not one of them. He had a face full of freckles and light hair. And to top it off, Eddie sounded like a country singer when he spoke in English. His southern drawl was difficult for Jenny to understand.

Back at the chalkboard, Ms. Candy wrote "FUN #2: VALENTINE'S DAY CELE-BRATION!!!" On the dot of each exclamation point Ms. Candy drew tiny hearts. "We will exchange valentines after the spelling bee. Remember our school rule—no store-bought cards! You must make each and every one yourself." The class began groaning and slinking, even more dramatically this time. "And, please do not sign your names," Ms. Candy continued as she danced around the classroom. "We may have some secret crushes in this class!"

As Jenny tried to figure out what a "crush" meant, Lilly whispered, "Tanner Capellini," as she stared longingly at the boy with blue eyes and long, dark hair on Jenny's other side. Jenny looked over at Tanner and he grinned back at her with a smile full of braces that made her face redden. Luckily, another teacher walked in from the shared fifth-grade office and saved it from burning to a crisp.

"I was just telling the class, Mr. Short, that there may be some secret crushes on Valentine's Day! Wouldn't you agree?" Ms. Candy asked him. Ms. Candy seemed to match her name perfectly, but as Mr. Short adjusted his big glasses, Jenny thought he seemed just the opposite of his name. He was actually very tall and skinny.

Staring dreamily into the distance, Ms. Candy continued to talk without letting Mr. Short answer. "Wouldn't it just be the bee's knees to have a date for Valentine's Day? Flowers, a romantic dinner, splittin' a double-layered chocolate cake for dessert, and—"

"Ms. Candy?" interrupted Mr. Short. He took out a small cloth from his shirt pocket and wiped the sweat from his face. Jenny looked at her own ruined shirt and felt relieved that someone else was feeling nervous. "Have you seen the spelling bee word lists?" he asked.

"Word lists?" asked Ms. Candy, her cheeks suddenly the same color as her hot pink lips. "Yes, of course," she said and walked over to her desk. As she handed a stack of paper to Mr. Short, she tripped over Aidan's backpack and all the word lists flew into the air. Both teachers tried furiously to catch them, but instead bumped right into each other. In the middle of all the commotion Lilly raised her hand. "Yes, Lilly?" asked Ms. Candy, as she peeled a page off the top of the world globe.

"It may be, like, impossible for me to like, finish, all my valentines on time because I have, like, four soccer practices a week," Lilly said. "Monday and Wednesday it's like, my regular team practice and Tuesday and Thursday is, like, my travel team. And Saturday is my game day and then I'm usually at like, a tournament or something on Sunday."

"Lilly," said Ms. Candy, "I had a hard time understanding what you said, but you did remind me of something else exciting that is happening in February."

Ms. Candy walked over to the chalkboard and wrote "FUN #3: FIFTH-GRADE SOCCER GAME." Jenny expected more moaning and slumping, but instead, the class cheered. Some students even stood on their chairs and danced. Jenny had never seen anything quite like it, especially in school.

"Mr. Short, our class hereby challenges your class to a soccer match for the ultimate prize—a whipped cream party!" shouted Ms. Candy, even louder than the students. Mr. Short tried to speak, but his quiet voice was lost among the noisy celebration. On his way out of the room, Mr. Short waved to Ms. Candy. And, because she was the only one who was actually paying attention, Jenny saw Ms. Candy wink back at him.

When the class settled down, Ms. Candy returned to the chalkboard. "Now, for two not-so-fun things," she said, sighing as she wrote "NOT-SO-FUN #1: SUGGESTION BOX." In the back row, Aidan snickered. "I encourage creative thinking," said Ms. Candy, "but someone in this class has been stuffing the suggestion box with silly ideas." A few boys laughed along with Aidan.

"Please remember to put only useful suggestions in the box. Those do not include handing out candy bars for snack or getting rid of math homework," said Ms. Candy. "And rest assured, we will never have a cartoon marathon in class, even on the last day of school." Nadia turned around and rolled her eyes at Aidan, who had a goofy grin on his face.

"And lastly," said Ms. Candy as she wrote down "NOT-SO-FUN #2: WRITING PROBLEM." Besides the time when Principal Brimstone had tried to make a joke, Jenny had not heard the class as quiet the entire morning, especially Aidan. "Let me remind you," Ms. Candy said in a much more serious voice, "that you are to write on paper only, and not on books or desks or walls. Destroying school property will result in a suspension that will be listed on your permanent school record. Does everyone, especially the person who has already ruined several classroom items, understand?"

"Yes, Ma'am," the class said in unison. For a brief moment, Jenny felt like she was back at one of her old Chinese-American schools.

At home that afternoon, Jenny lay on her bed thinking about her first day at Haverswell Elementary. She was supposed to be doing homework or practicing piano but instead, she was drawing comics, the thing she loved to do most. By the third move, Jenny had figured out that her family would never be anywhere for too long and she decided that it really wasn't worth the effort to make friends. By the time Jenny got close to anyone, it was time to leave again. Jenny's only real friends were the characters who lived in her comics. They stuck around.

"Jenny?" Mrs. Liu called from the kitchen.

"Yes, Mommy?" answered Jenny.

"I don't hear piano," said Mrs. Liu. "You practice."

"I'm studying, Mommy," Jenny lied as she sketched the next panel of her comic.

"Jenny, you practice now," said Mrs. Liu. Jenny was so absorbed that she didn't notice that her mother had walked into her room. Quickly, Jenny hid her notebook under the pillow. "Drawing is waste of time," Mrs. Liu said, as she handed Jenny a piano book from the bookshelf. Pointing at the electronic piano, Mrs. Liu said, "Piano good."

Jenny sulked all the way from her bed to the piano bench. With fingers blackened by drawing pencil smudges, she began practicing her scales.

TUESDAY, FEBRUARY 2:
SHORT AND SWEET

Airborne biscuit crumbs, a teacher that looked like cotton candy, yelling, burping, hugging, moaning, flying worksheets, dancing on chairs. Jenny sat quietly at her desk and watched the rest of the class file in, certain that nothing could top the craziness of her first day at Haverswell Elementary. As soon as Ms. Candy arrived, however, Jenny quickly changed her mind.

"FWEEEEEEEEEEEE!" rang Ms. Candy's whistle as she stepped into the classroom. Immediately, everyone came to attention. Even Aidan looked alive in the back. "Time for Tuesday Times Tables! TIME for Tuesday TIMES Tables!" Ms. Candy sang as she marched around the room in knee-high black boots twirling a baton. She was dressed in a pink skirt, a ruffled white blouse and a two-foot-tall pink hat with a giant yellow feather. Jenny smiled to herself, remembering the pretty majorettes that she had watched dance with the marching bands in The Rose Bowl Parade when she lived in California. Ms. Candy would have fit right in. As Ms. Candy strutted past her chair, Jenny noticed that her hat was covered with numbers and guessed that the Tuesday morning commotion probably had something to do with math. Math and majorettes.

"Good morning, class!" beamed Ms. Candy. "Let's get into our Tuesday Times Tables rows!" Everyone scurried like mice to change seats with the exception of Nadia, who stayed put in the front and Aidan, who didn't budge from the back. Jenny didn't know what to do, so she stayed right where she was, too, in the middle of her row.

"Remember, the easiest math problem will go to the person in the back seat and the hardest one will go to the person in the front seat," said Ms. Candy. "FWEEEEEEEEEEEE!" She blew her whistle again. "Ten seconds to make your final order changes before the race starts!" she said, marching to the head of the class as she rolled the baton back and forth along her elbow. Mesmerized by the baton routine, Jenny didn't notice Lilly standing next to her until she felt a tap on her shoulder.

"Jenny," Lilly said. "Your row, like, wants you to move up to, like, the front." When Jenny didn't respond, Lilly pulled her up and added, "Quick! Like, switch with Tyler. It's almost time to start!" Tyler took Jenny's seat in the middle while Jenny walked slowly to the front and reluctantly sat down.

Ms. Candy placed a math worksheet on each desk in the back. "Why do we have to do the times tables races every single Tuesday?" Aidan moaned. There were a few similar grumbles from around the room.

Nadia looked back at Aidan and stuck her nose in the air. "Some of us actually like to practice math, Aidan," she said.

Aidan leaned back in his chair and said, "Better put your nose down, Nadia, or a bird might land on it and make a nest!" Jenny didn't understand what Aidan said, but it must have been funny because the class burst into laughter.

Nadia crossed her arms and said, "We'll see which row wins, won't we?"

"Don't pitch a fit, y'all," said Ms. Candy. She tossed the baton high into the air and caught it behind her back. "This is gonna be fun!" When Ms. Candy blew her whistle and yelled, "Go!" the students in the back flipped over the worksheet and furiously began to solve their assigned math problem. The worksheets were passed seat by seat toward the front as each person finished. Jenny felt herself getting excited. Her row was in the lead.

Nadia, on the other hand, seemed worried and kept mouthing, "Faster!" to everyone behind her.

Jenny felt another tap on her shoulder. When she turned around, a serious-looking girl with glasses handed her the worksheet and with a look that meant business said, "Get 'er done."

$$3 \times (6 \times 2) + 4 \times 4 = ?$$

Jenny studied the math problem and all at once she felt the enthusiasm drain out of her. She couldn't remember any times tables. The more Jenny tried the more she panicked, especially when Tyler cheered, "We're so going to win! Jenny's a total math genius!" But, Jenny could barely pick up her pencil. She had never been that great at math. Plus, all the numbers blended into one big blur on the page. All Jenny managed to do was draw an unhappy face for the answer and play with her long braids until the other rows finished.

While Ms. Candy checked the calculations at her desk, the class returned to their seats and waited anxiously for the results. Finally, she announced, "Nadia's row wins again!" Aidan groaned loudly.

Nadia beamed as she accepted the prizes, Haverswell Hawks erasers. As she handed them to her row, she smirked at Aidan and mouthed, "Told you so."

"What? We totally had it in the bag!" yelled Tyler. "What happened?"

Jenny tried to conceal her embarrassment by looking down at her desk but when she did, she noticed a note that read, "TO: JENNY" and she blushed even more. Jenny hid the note under her desk and attempted to fold it open slowly without anyone noticing, especially Ms. Candy. Note-passing was forbidden in Jenny's former Chinese-American schools, not that she ever had any friends to break the rules with. Jenny snuck a quick look at the note. Three words were written down. "IT'S ALL GOOD." Quickly, Jenny crumbled up the paper and stuffed it in her pocket. Ms. Candy blew her whistle again, leaving Jenny with no time to figure out who the message was from.

"I'm fixin' to have a snack in a minute. All that twirling has got me hungrier than a hound dog!" laughed Ms. Candy. She removed her majorette's hat and brushed the hair off her forehead. "Why don't y'all get some water before we go out for recess? I'll eat my apple."

Jenny stayed seated while the class raced toward the hallway water fountain. Tuesday Times Tables had made her thirsty, but she was too afraid of being caught with the note to move. Jenny watched quietly as Ms. Candy reached into the paper bag on her desk and pulled out a donut that was covered with pink icing and rainbow sprinkles. She took a big bite and licked her lips. As Ms. Candy took another humongous bite, she turned around toward the students' desks and let out a squeal when she noticed Jenny. With a mouth-full of donut she mumbled, "I didn't know you were here." Ms. Candy quickly dropped the donut back into the paper bag, which she then shoved into her desk drawer while Jenny pretended to read a textbook.

Ms. Candy wiped her sugary hands onto her blouse, grabbed one of the math worksheets off her desk and walked toward Jenny. "Jenny, we need to talk about something," she said, pointing to the unhappy face Jenny had drawn during the math race. Just then, kids started returning. Jenny felt her throat close up and her heart begin to race, and she was confident that the entire class would witness her telling-off. Jenny imagined that Ms. Candy would empty her pockets and discover the secret note, which meant she would not only be humiliated, but that she would have to endure Principal Brimstone again.

But all Ms. Candy did was lean toward her desk and whisper, "Sit in the back next time." Jenny smiled at Ms. Candy, not in her usual polite way, but fully, with her whole heart, as if to say, "Thank you for understanding." Ms. Candy winked back at her and for the first time in her life, Jenny realized what it felt like to want to hug someone she barely knew.

The class lined up for recess, but instead of going outside, Ms. Candy put back on her pink majorette hat, hopped to the front of the room and starting blowing her whistle again. "FWEEEEEEEEEEEE!" She pointed her baton toward the shared fifth-grade office and shouted, "Forward march!" The class began to high step, following Ms. Candy through the office. As they entered Mr. Short's classroom, she twirled the baton above her head and began to sing, "I don't know but I've been told."

Without missing a beat, the class repeated in unison, "I don't know but I've been told."

Mr. Short's students watched Ms. Candy's class march around the room, their mouths hung wide open as if they were catching flies. Mr. Short, however, just sat at his desk and grinned. He seemed to accept that the performance was simply Ms. Candy being Ms. Candy.

"Ms. Candy's class can score the goals!" shouted Ms. Candy.

The class repeated, "Ms. Candy's class can score the goals!"

Although she didn't sing along or cheer with the rest of the class, Jenny's legs marched, her arms swung back and forth, and noise filled her ears. When Lilly danced or Tyler gestured "number one" with his finger or Ms. Candy twirled her baton, Jenny, herself, felt energized. She was used to watching parades. Now she felt like she was part of one.

The line looped around the classroom one more time. Ms. Candy yelled, "Company, halt!" and the class came to a standstill. But, Aidan wasn't concentrating and bumped right into Nadia, who then stumbled into a desk. Flustered, Nadia stared angrily at Aidan, who, happy with the accidental attention, laughed along with everyone else. Nadia adjusted her hair bow and brushed her shirt disgustedly, as if Aidan had just infected her with some rare disease.

"Ms. Candy!" cried Nadia, tears beginning to fall.

Without a fight, Ms. Candy sent Nadia to the nurse's office and then began twirling her baton again. "Sound off!" she yelled.

The class shouted back, "One, two!" Twirling the baton faster and faster, Ms. Candy yelled, "Sound off!"

The class shouted back, "Three, four!"

"Sound off, one, two, three, four," she continued.

By this time, Ms. Candy's baton was turning so quickly that it looked like she was holding spinning helicopter blades. Suddenly, she tossed it up. Jenny felt the entire room hold their breath as the baton landed, still spinning, onto the middle of her back. Lilly high-fived Tyler as he yelled out, "Epic!" A few students had begun to clap for what they thought was the finale when Ms. Candy unexpectedly leaned into a cartwheel, causing the baton to fly back into the air.

Ms. Candy caught the baton flat-handed and she shouted, "We're gonna be the fifth-grade soccer champs!" The room roared with applause and for the third time that morning, Jenny smiled for real.

Mr. Short tried to inspire his class with a "Go Mr. Short's class!" cheer, but even his most forceful voice was no match for a room of rowdy fifth graders and a baton-twirling teacher.

"Ms. Candy, that was, well, you...," mumbled Mr. Short, adjusting his glasses.

"What?" she yelled back.

"You definitely...," he started again, but then he shook his head in defeat. The class was much too loud.

Ms. Candy tapped her baton a few times on the desk and when the class still didn't quiet down, she picked up her whistle and blew it as loud as she could, silencing the class in an instant. "What were you saying, Mr. Short?" she asked.

"Ms. Candy...," Mr. Short started quietly, his hands buried in his pockets, his eyes unable to look up at her all the way.

Ms. Candy smiled encouragingly and asked, "Yes, Mr. Short?"

"I was just saying that you...you definitely march to the beat of a different drummer, Ms. Candy!" Mr. Short managed.

"Darlin', you don't get to be Miss South Carolina without having some kinda talent!" she laughed back at him. "I'm no spring chicken, Mr. Short, but I've still got the moves. That's what healthy eating will do for you!" Eyeing the shiny red apple on his desk, she said, "Actually, I just had an apple, my-self!"

At that moment, Jenny noticed a big clump of sprinkles on Ms. Candy's shirt where she had wiped her hands after she hid the donut. Jenny couldn't stop staring at the sprinkles. Like a bright rainbow neon sign they flashed, "I DIDN'T EAT AN APPLE. I ATE A SUGARY DONUT," over and over. Jenny had already caught Ms. Candy lying about her snack earlier and now she was be-ing untruthful again, this time in front of Mr. Short and all the fifth graders. Jenny's heart began to race.

As Ms. Candy lined up the class to go out-side for recess, Jenny remembered how many times she had lied to her mother about study-ing or practicing piano. Jenny wondered if Ms. Candy felt the same way about healthy food as she did about the things she hated. Maybe Ms. Candy loved donuts as much as she loved her comics. Suddenly, Jenny lunged toward Ms. Candy, wrapping her arms awkwardly around her teacher's waist. She didn't let go until she had completely wiped off the sprinkles.

Ms. Candy almost fell over and with a look of bewilderment, chuckled gently at Jenny. "Well, aren't you as sweet as a honey bee!" she said. Jenny stepped back into line between Lilly and Tyler, who seemed to neither notice nor care because they were too busy arguing about who would score more goals in the soccer game. "Alight, y'all! Let's head out to the playground," said Ms. Candy. "Bye, Mr. Short's class! See you at the Fifth-Grade Soccer Game!" Ms. Candy added as she led the class out the door.

So far, everything about Haverswell Elementary seemed loud to Jenny, especially the cafeteria. At lunch, most of the fifth grade kids sat in groups, sharing pizza and chicken nuggets, and talking and laughing. Jenny sat alone eating the noodles and vegetables she had brought from home, remembering how she had felt just as lonely at her old Chinese-American schools. Jenny had sat next to other kids, but it wasn't because she was friends with them, it was only because the lunchroom was so crowded.

The only other person at Jenny's table was Mr. Short, who sat on the other end by himself. He was supposed to be monitoring lunch but instead he was lost deep in a book. Jenny watched him crunch the red apple that Ms. Candy had pointed out on his desk. As he turned the pages, he spooned vegetable soup from a metal thermos and occasionally took sips from a water bottle. Jenny wondered if Mr. Short's healthiness was the reason Ms. Candy lied about eating the donut.

When Mr. Short had finished his lunch, he walked up to the vending machine and dug out some change from his pockets. Jenny was convinced that he would buy another water bottle for the afternoon or maybe a bag of whole wheat crackers, but what popped out was a package of two chocolate cupcakes topped with chocolate and swirls of vanilla icing. Back at the lunch table, Jenny pretended to eat her noodles while she watched Mr. Short gobble up every single bite of his cupcakes, including the gooey filling. Jenny guessed that Mr. Short liked a little sweetness in his life after all.

When lunch was over, Mr. Short walked the fifth graders back to their classrooms. Ms. Candy had changed out of her majorette outfit and was busy covering the chalkboard with spelling words, which caused the mood to change from cheerful to gloomy the instant the kids figured out what was going on. Jenny hoped that whatever happened didn't involve speed races.

Ms. Candy announced that the class would be taking a practice test for the upcoming spelling bee. Jenny relaxed. Spelling words in front of people was difficult, but due to years of memorizing the dictionary when she was first learning to speak English, she usually got them correct if she was able to write them down.

In the middle of the test, just after Ms. Candy had called out the word "deceive," Nadia began shrieking. "Ms. Candy! Ms. Candy!" she yelled. "Someone wrote on my eraser!"

Ms. Candy took a deep breath and said, "Pencils down, class." No one moved. No one said a word.

Nadia held up her Haverswell Hawks eraser and cried, "It's not fair!" as she handed it to Ms. Candy. "I forgot that 'e' came before the 'i' in 'deceive' and when I reached for my eraser, I saw the graffiti!"

As she walked over to examine the evidence Ms. Candy said, "Can everyone in Nadia's row please take out their new Haverswell Hawks erasers?" Sure enough, every single one was covered with black marker. With this news, Nadia began slamming her fists down on her desk and crying uncontrollably. Ms. Candy put a hand on

Nadia's shoulder to try and calm her down, but it caused her to cry even louder.

"It's just a stupid eraser," said Aidan. Jenny noticed that she wasn't the only one who gasped at his insensitive comment.

Before Ms. Candy had a chance to respond, Nadia turned around and with a face wet with tears she screamed, "Oh yeah? Well, you probably did it, Aidan!"

Ms. Candy held up a handful of ruined erasers and in the most serious tone Jenny had heard from her yet said, "Aidan, you best take a trip see Principal Brimstone."

That afternoon, Jenny started her homework, but gave up after only a few minutes because she found it hard to concentrate with a mind full of the day's activities. As she took out her drawing notebook instead, she smiled and floated into the pages.

"Jenny?" Mrs. Liu called from the kitchen.

"Yes, Mommy?" answered Jenny.

"You studying?" asked Mrs. Liu.

"Yes, Mommy," Jenny said, sighing as she put away her notebook and picked up her math homework. As much as Jenny loved to draw, she had already heard enough lies that day.

WEDNESDAY, FEBRUARY 3:
THE WRITING ON THE WALL

By the time Ms. Candy's class came back from lunch at 1 o'clock that afternoon, Aidan had already been sent to Principal Brimstone's office three times. Between visits, he was either slumped in his chair like a lazy sloth, curtains of long bangs draping his eyes as if he was half-asleep, or as Ms. Candy had declared, fidgeting like he had "ants in his pants." Jenny had never heard this expression before, but because she could easily imagine hundreds of ants crawling up and down Aidan's legs whenever he squirmed in his chair or kicked the desk or let out a dramatic sigh as he chewed his pencil, she loved it immediately.

Aidan's first prank happened in the beginning of the day when Ms. Candy called the class over for Morning Meeting. The sportier boys were walking over to their usual spot on the carpet when Jack yelled, "I didn't know how much you loved mermaids, dude!" to Tyler just before he sat down.

If the wisecrack flustered Tyler, he certainly didn't show it. He pointed to the mascot on his maroon football jersey and said mockingly, "Dude, that's not a mermaid. It's a Fighting Gamecock."

"C-A-R-O-L-I-N-A! Fight. Fight. GoooOOOOOOO Gamecocks!" the class suddenly exploded in unison.

Jenny sat very still in her space on the carpet, unsure of what was happening and what would come next. Some of the boys did touchdown victory dances. Ms. Candy began jumping up and down excitedly. Jenny hoped she would start marching around the classroom and twirling the baton again.

Instead, she folded her three middle fingers down and extended her thumb and pinky, then shook her wrist back and forth while yelling, "So, let's give a cheer! Carolina is here!"

Copying Ms. Candy's hand gesture, the class answered with, "C-A-R-O-L-I-N-A! Fight. Fight. GoooOOOOOOO Gamecocks!"

As he high-fived Jack, Tyler shook his head in disbelief and said, "South Carolina? You know, one of the top ten teams in college football?" Then he added, "Duh. You should know that! We've only watched every game together since we were five!"

Jack said, "Dude, not your shirt. I mean there's a mermaid on your jeans!" Before Tyler could figure out exactly what was going on, a ripple of laughter spread throughout the room.

Pointing to Tyler's bottom, Lilly said, "Sorry to tell you this, Ty, but you do, like, have a giant mermaid on, like, your butt cheek!"

Tyler felt his bottom and yelled, "What the...?" Agitated, he began furiously peeling off stickers from the back of his jeans. The class giggled as Tyler discovered not only a mermaid, but several princesses, butterflies and flowers.

Aidan let out a loud belly laugh. Most of the time, if Aidan found something funny the class laughed right along. This time, because Tyler was the target of his prank, not even one person dared to chuckle.

Tyler glared at Aidan with eyes full of fire. It was the first time all week that Jenny had seen him lose his cool. "Were you the idiot who put these girly stickers on my chair, sticky-side up?" he asked pointedly.

Aidan shrugged his shoulders. Ms. Candy looked sternly at Aidan and asked, "Aidan, did you put the stickers on Tyler's chair?" But again, Aidan only shrugged his shoulders. "Well, Aidan, if you can't tell me that you didn't, then I'm going to assume you did."

Ms. Candy got up from her rocking chair. As she walked toward her desk, she put a hand on Tyler's shoulder and said, "Oh, honey, you've still got a giant pink heart on your left backside." Tyler quickly pulled it off and proceeded to rip it to shreds while he and the sporty boys glared at Aidan.

Ms. Candy called Aidan to her desk and handed him a piece of paper. "Give this to Principal Brimstone," she said. Aidan moped toward the door, his head hung gloomily toward the floor, without looking back at anyone.

To get ready for the Fifth-Grade Soccer Game, Coach Adkins brought Ms. Candy's class outside for field practice. Aidan, who was back from the principal's office, was gasping for breath in the first few minutes of the game and proceeded to collapse onto the grass. He looked relieved at a chance to rest unbothered. Nadia refused to step onto the field because she didn't want to ruin her new dress.

Lilly and Tyler were put on the same team, which meant that no one else got much playing time. Lilly would dribble the ball and pass it to Tyler, who would run around everyone else, even his own teammates. When Tyler found Lilly waiting in front of the goal, he would tap over a quick pass. In one touch, Lilly would shoot the ball like a blasting rocket toward whatever victim was goalkeeper. All Coach Adkins could do to rally the class was yell out, "Look alive! Y'all are slower than a herd of turtles!"

The one time that the dynamic duo didn't score was when Coach Adkins put Jenny in goal. Jenny, who had never played soccer in her life, ran toward Lilly's attempt, tripped over her own foot and landed on the ball. Coach Adkins cheered, "You've got it, Jenny!" But, Jenny knew she didn't have anything but dumb luck and on the next several shots, she was either hit in the face, dropped the ball or misjudged its angle completely. Jenny did manage to stop the ball once more, but then somehow ended up kicking it into her own goal, scoring on herself.

After soccer practice, the class trooped in to use the hallway water fountain before heading back into the classroom. And that's when Aidan's second prank happened. Nadia, who hadn't even broken a sweat, who still had every hair perfectly in place, pushed her way right past Lilly and Tyler to the front of the line. When she pressed the button to take a drink, the water shot up into her eye. Nadia started to let out a little scream, but when she heard Lilly and Tyler giggling, she stopped. Nadia tried to take another drink, but this time, the water sprayed her dress. Even though she pressed the button over and over again, she couldn't get it to stop. In a matter of seconds, Nadia was soaked. Soaked and hysterically crying.

All the commotion sent both Ms. Candy and Mr. Short out of their classrooms in a panic. Ms. Candy slipped on the puddle of water in her high heels. She came within inches of sliding right into the wall, but was saved when Mr. Short's long arms pulled her back to safety. Without skipping a beat, Ms. Candy reached into the water fountain and pulled a twig out of the spout. She shook her head as she handed it to Mr. Short and said, "Classic." Mr. Short grinned back at her. Then, Ms. Candy walked up to Aidan and said, "Did you rig the water fountain?" Aidan just shrugged his shoulders. Ms. Candy smoothed back her matted wet bangs, wiped the mascara from under her eyes and sighed back, "Principal Brimstone's office." Without saying a word, Aidan started down the hall-way.

Aidan's antics, the football cheers, and Ms. Candy's near crash had made for an eventful morning. From her head to her feet, Jenny still ached from getting smacked by the soc-cer ball so many times. She was actually re-lieved to have a quiet lunch period by herself. As Jenny surveyed the contents of her lunch box, a paper bag rustled from the other end of the table, which reminded her that she wasn't quite alone. Mr. Short had been her sole lunch companion all week. But Jenny didn't mind. He was as quiet as she was. Then, from out of nowhere, a plastic lunch tray came crashing down on the table, causing Jenny's rice to pop up from its container and Mr. Short's vegetable soup to swan dive out of the side of his bowl. With similar force, Aidan plopped himself down onto a seat in the middle of the table. Jenny looked up and Aidan mumbled, "Can I sit here?"

Partly because she was scared of Aidan, but mostly because she was shy, Jenny shrugged her shoulders. "Well, if you don't tell me that I can't, then I'm going to assume I can," Aidan said, imitating Ms. Candy. Mr. Short, who was watching the whole scene, nodded his approval. For the remainder of lunch, the trio sat in almost-silence, the only noises an occasional slurp or chew or clink of silverware. Toward the end of the period, Aidan got up to clear his tray. Mr. Short got up to visit the vending machine and returned with his daily cupcakes. And, that's when Aidan's third prank took place.

Minutes later, a large crowd had formed around the lunch room sink. Jenny turned around to see several shrieking kids running toward her table. As they got closer, Jenny realized that their hands were completely covered in purple dye. Mr. Short had just sunk his teeth into the last bite of frosting and took his time swallowing it down before he examined their purple hands. Sighing, he got up from the table and scanned the lunch-room until he found Aidan, who was hiding behind the trash can.

Mr. Short walked up to him and asked, "Purple food coloring in the soap dispenser?" Aidan shrugged his shoulders. This time, because he was the official lunch monitor, Mr. Short was the one to send Aidan to Principal Brimstone's office.

After lunch, the music teacher, Ms. El-lison, was attempting to teach Ms. Candy's class one of South Carolina's state songs. To kick off the soccer game, all the fifth graders would be singing together in front of their parents, a fact that Ms. Ellison tried to scare them with every time they forgot the words. Because Jenny had been playing piano for almost as long as she could walk, memorizing songs came easily. By the third time around, Jenny had learned the tune and almost all the words. Music class was nearly finished, but the students had only managed to make it through the first verse of the song without their voices starting to fade out. "This is an official song of South Carolina! Y'all should know every word!" Ms. Ellison said. "Feel it in your heart! South Carolina pride!"

Before they started again, Ms. Candy peeked into the music room and frowned when she realized that Nadia was the only one singing the beginning of second verse. Jenny felt herself frown, too. She couldn't wait for the second line, her favorite of the whole song, because she found particular delight in rhyming the English words "beaches" and "peaches," at least in her head. At home the previous evening, Jenny had been pleasantly surprised to read that South Carolina had lots of beautiful beaches, just like California. Her state history book had also mentioned that peaches were South Carolina's state fruit. She now understood why sliced peaches were the only fruit the Haverswell Elementary cafeteria served. This realization made Jenny think of her favorite Ms. Candy expression so far, "Slap my head and call me silly!" She liked it a whole lot better than "duh," which most of her classmates seemed to prefer.

Ms. Candy started to sing in what Jenny noted was perfect pitch. "Our state has rivers, lakes, an ocean. It's got our true devotion. Oh, South Carolina pride!" But, she suddenly stopped and cried, "Oh, sugar, I forgot about Aidan!" Ms. Candy turned to Nadia and said, "Nadia, please go get Aidan from Principal Brimstone's office."

"Yes, Ma'am," Nadia said as she walked away looking smug.

Ms. Ellison on the other hand, looked defeated. She sighed, "The only one who actually knows the words just walked out the door!"

After Nadia left, Ms. Candy said to the class, "Y'all, Aidan sure is getting my goose today, but it IS his birthday." She looked at the clock and said, "Shoot, I gotta go get ready!" She skipped toward the door and yelled back, "Keep singing!"

A few minutes later, Aidan walked in and snuck into the back row. The class still had not made it through the second verse. Ms. Ellison asked desperately, "What comes after 'Oh, South Carolina pride'?"

Jenny wanted to scream out the answer, "Our state has mountains, it has beaches. It's got Foothills, juicy peaches. Oh, South Carolina pride!" But, she didn't say a word. Unfortunately, neither did anyone else.

Ms. Ellison sighed. "Aidan, where's Nadia?"

Aidan mumbled, "She had to go to the bathroom."

Ms. Ellison sighed again. "From the top of the second verse, please!" she said. The class started to sing and once again, they didn't make it past the first line. This time, however, it wasn't because they forgot the words. Ms. Candy had sailed into the room on roller skates holding a pizza box.

"Special delivery for Aidan!" Ms. Candy announced. "I know you're not having the best day, but maybe this will make it a little bit better." The class turned to look at Aidan. "And now for a song y'all DO know," Ms. Candy said to the class. She led them in a melancholy rendition of "Happy Birthday" as Aidan stared at the wall. For someone who was used to getting all sorts of attention, Jenny thought he seemed embarrassed.

"Happy Birthday, Aidan!" Ms. Candy declared cheerfully. But when she opened the pizza box, she let out a gasp. The box didn't contain a pizza, but a giant cookie decorated to look like one. The crust was a sugar cookie and the tomato sauce was made of red frosting. Squirts of white frosting were supposed to resemble shredded cheese and strawberry fruit rolls had been cut up into pepperoni shapes. It was the most disgusting thing Jenny had ever seen.

"Well, ain't that the berries!" Ms. Candy exclaimed. "Did your momma make that?"

"My step-mom," Aidan said sharply.

Ms. Candy put her hand on Aidan's shoulder and smiled, "I reckon I've never seen such a thing! Please tell her it's a true work of art!" Aidan just rolled his eyes. Ms. Candy looked knowingly at Ms. Ellison and said, "We'll enjoy some cake back in the classroom, but only when y'all can figure out that second verse!" Although the class moaned, the reward seemed to make them snap to attention.

Just then, Nadia returned. As she squeezed next to her in the front row, Jenny couldn't help noticing that Nadia's dress was not only wet again, but that the front was spotted with black smudges. Nadia caught her staring and folded her arms tightly around her dress. As she gave Aidan the evil eye in the back row, she whispered to Jenny, "I think the water fountain is still broken."

Ms. Ellison started the song again. This time, not only Nadia, but both Tyler and Lilly, belted out the words. Ms. Candy was tearing up. Tanner kept the beat with his foot. And when the class got to the second verse, everyone finally remembered the words.

Jenny wasn't sure if everyone had pizza cook-ie cake or South Carolina pride on their minds, but she, Ms. Ellison and Ms. Candy all smiled, relieved that the class had finally managed to make it through the song.

Back in the classroom, Ms. Candy cut up Aidan's pizza cookie cake. She passed out the slices and told the students that before they were allowed to take a bite, they had to do a math exercise and measure its area. "Take out your rulers," she said. The students reached into their desks and all of a sudden, a hush came over the room. Jenny looked down at her ruler, which was covered with black marker, just like everyone else's.

Ms. Candy called for Mr. Short and in a matter of seconds, he came running in. When he saw the rulers, he shook his head. "Unbe-lievable," he said, looking at Aidan.

"On a more positive note, we were just about to have a birthday treat!" Ms. Candy laughed. "Would you like a slice?"

Mr. Short looked distastefully at the pizza cookie cake and as politely as possible said, "No, thank you."

"I'm just pickin' with ya," Ms. Candy laughed nervously. "It looks pretty gross, doesn't it?" Mr. Short nodded his head in agreement while Jenny noticed Ms. Candy trying to hide a half-eaten slice behind her back. Then Nadia screamed and both teachers rushed over to see what had happened.

"Ewww! It's all over my new dress!" Nadia cried, pointing out the black marks. "My dad just got this for me! Now it's ruined, just like the rulers!"

Mr. Short comforted Nadia and Ms. Candy said, "Aidan, please come up to my desk." As Aidan approached, Ms. Candy said, "Gather your things to go home. Principal Brimstone will call your dad and your step-mom."

This time, Aidan didn't shrug his shoulders. He argued, "But, I didn't do it!"

Ms. Candy said, "Aidan, first the stickers, then the water fountain and then the purple dye. And, now you are destroying school supplies."

"Ms. Candy, I didn't write on the rulers!" Aidan pleaded.

Ms. Candy looked at him sorrowfully. "I hope your birthday party won't be ruined by this bad day," she said.

Aidan snapped, "Birthday parties are for babies." On his way back to get his things, he looked at Nadia and under his breath he said, "And besides, parents don't let their kids hang out with me anymore. I'm a bad influence, right, Nadia?"

Nadia cringed, folding her arms tightly around her dress. Jenny remembered that Nadia had done exactly the same thing in music class when she was trying to hide the black marks. "Slap my head and call me silly!" Jenny thought. Things were starting to make sense.

In her bedroom after school, Jenny was on her computer playing videos of the South Carolina song. Her earphones were in and she was singing more loudly than she realized.

Only when Jenny felt her long hair being smoothed did she notice that her mother had come in. Jenny pulled out her earphones and turned around.

"It's for school, Mommy," Jenny said.

"School?" Jenny's mother asked, studying the video.

"It's homework, Mommy," Jenny said.

"Okay, okay," said Jenny's mother. As she walked out of the room she added, "Do homework."

Jenny played the music video one more time even though she already knew the South Carolina state song by heart. Then as quietly as she could, Jenny took out her notebook and began to draw.

THURSDAY, FEBRUARY 4:
OUT OF, LIKE, PLAY

"Well," Lilly announced loudly, throwing up her arms in defeat as she walked into the classroom, "we might as well, like, kiss the whole, like, whipped cream party goodbye!"

Ms. Candy, who was in the middle of writing the day's schedule on the chalkboard in bright orange, looked confused. She said, "I didn't quite understand you, Lilly. Could you repeat that?"

In one move, Lilly fell into her chair, flung her head back and planted her feet on the desk. All week she had worn shiny track pants in various color combinations—blue and green, black and red, purple and white— always with a coordinated top. Today's uniform consisted of teal and yellow striped pants paired with a grey shirt that bragged "EAT, SLEEP, PLAY SOCCER" in huge letters. After Lilly's amazing performance in yesterday's soccer practice, Jenny didn't doubt the shirt's claim. She did, however, think that "TALK" should be added to the list because in the three days that Jenny had sat next to Lilly, soccer seemed to be her favorite topic of conversation.

Lilly repeated, "We might as well, like, kiss the whole, like, whipped cream party, like, goodbye!"

Ms. Candy continued to look confused. She put down her chalk and dusted her hands onto her skirt. Because the material was a pattern of neon-colored waves, it blended right in. With her hands on her hips, Ms. Candy said to Lilly, "First things first. Those dirty sneakers need to walk themselves off the desk and onto the floor where they belong." Huffing and puffing, Lilly dropped her long legs dramatically off the desk causing her sneakers to hit the floor with a bang. Then all of a sudden, Lilly buried her head into her arms on the desk. Her blonde French braid bobbed up and down with each heavy breath. "Second," Ms. Candy continued, "I'm about as lost as last year's Easter egg. Can someone please explain to me what Lilly's sayin' and why she's so upset?"

Tyler immediately piped up. "Basically, Lilly said that our class is going to lose the Fifth-Grade Soccer Game, which means we won't get to have the whipped cream party," he explained.

Ms. Candy said, "But Coach Adkins told me you and Lilly were goin' whole hog in soccer practice yesterday. Wasn't the final score fifteen to one?"

From her arm cave Lilly moaned, "Sixteen to one."

Jack asked, "Are you sick?"

Lilly groaned, "No."

Jack asked, "Are you injured?"

Without lifting her head, Lilly yelled, "Like, no!" and then she stomped the ground in frustration.

Ms. Candy said, "Okay, Jack, that's enough," as she walked toward Lilly. Then she put her head down next to Lilly's and whispered, "Even the toughest nails in the toolbox bend from time to time. Go on and have a good ol' cry." With Ms. Candy's go-ahead, Lilly began to sob. After a few minutes, Ms. Candy began to look concerned and asked, "What is it, honey?"

Lilly slowly lifted up her head. Her usually cheerful face was covered with red blotches and her blue eyes were sad and puffy from crying. Lilly said glumly, "Apparently, I'm, like, a bad influence or something."

Aidan, who had been oddly quiet, perhaps as a result of yesterday's many visits to the principal's office or maybe because Nadia was out sick, shouted, "I know how that feels!"

Ms. Candy looked at him sternly and said, "Let's let Lilly finish, Aidan." She turned to comfort Lilly and said, "Honey, in my book, you're the furthest thing from a bad influence."

"Yeah, well, like, tell that to my, like, parents!" Lilly said. "They think I'm, like, damaging my baby sister or something just by, like, like, talking!" Even though Ms. Candy was only two inches away from Lilly, she had to concentrate with all her might to understand what Lilly was saying. Lilly continued, "And, like, now, I, like, have to go to some, like, speech evaluation, all because of her, like, one word."

"One word?" Ms. Candy asked.

"Like, one word!" Lilly cried.

"I don't get it," said Jack.

"Like, her first word!" Lilly said.

"I still don't get it," said Jack. Ms. Candy looked back at him with her finger pressed to her lips.

"Last night, she, like, finally said, like, her first word," Lilly sighed.

Turning to Lilly, Ms. Candy asked, "Let me get this straight. Your baby sister said her first word last night and your parents are not very happy about that particular word." Lilly nodded her head.

Aidan asked excitedly, "Oh, man, is it a bad word?" Then, with a mischievous smile on his face, he added, "Three or four letters?"

Lilly said, "It's, like, four letters, but it isn't, like, bad or anything!"

"I don't get it," said Jack.

"If it's not a bad word, you're welcome to share it with the class," said Ms. Candy.

"Tell us! Tell us!" Aidan encouraged her.

Lilly buried her head in her arms again and moaned, "Like!"

"Sounds like what?" asked Jack.

Lilly lifted up her head and said, "Like!"

"I don't get it," said Jack. Raising her eyebrows at him, Ms. Candy made a shushing noise.

"I think I understand," Ms. Candy said sweetly. "Was 'like' your baby sister's first word?" Lilly managed to nod through a new round of tears. "Oh, honey," said Ms. Candy as she put an arm around her shoulder.

Aidan yelled out, "Awwwww, man! That was totally disappointing!" He slumped into his chair and said, "Ugh. 'Like' isn't even a bad word!"

Ms. Candy ignored Aidan. She looked at Lilly affectionately and asked, "Are your parents sending you to speech lessons to get you to stop saying 'like' so much?" Lilly nodded again. "And, is your speech evaluation scheduled at the same exact time as the Fifth-Grade Soccer Game?"

Lilly said, "Uh huh."

"Now I get it," said Jack. "Lilly's gonna miss the game."

Frowning, Tyler said miserably, "And, I'm out of the best scoring partner around."

Lilly turned around to face Tyler and wiping her eyes she said, "I'm sorry, Ty. I'm, like, so sorry!" Lilly pounded the desk. "See! I can't, like, stop saying 'like'!" she screamed, punching herself in the arm in disgust.

Ms. Candy patted Lilly on the head and said, "You must feel like you've been chewed up and spit out." She walked up to the chalkboard and turning around to face the class, she smiled encouragingly and asked, "You ever seen a new lamb learn to walk?" A few of the kids raised their hands. Ms. Candy continued, "My granddaddy always used to ask me this question when I wanted to give up on somethin'." She let out a little laugh. "See, sometimes, it takes a while for a baby lamb to get up on his feet and figure out the whole walking thing. He's gonna fall, that's for sure. But, he just keeps tryin' and gettin' himself back up. And, you know what? Eventually, that baby lamb is out there hoofing it with the rest of the flock!"

"I don't get it," said Jack. "What does a baby lamb have to do with Lilly saying 'like' too much?

Ms. Candy smiled. "You will stop saying 'like' so much, Lilly. You might just have to get as serious about speaking practice as you are about soccer practice, that's all."

Tyler argued, "But, the soccer game is in eight days. Lilly doesn't have enough time!" The class began to grumble in agreement.

Ms. Candy said, "Stranger things have happened," and she turned toward the chalkboard to finish writing down the day's activities.

Jenny sat quietly in her seat as the rest of the class continued to discuss how Lilly's absence would affect the Fifth-Grade Soccer Game. Tyler, Jack and their group strategized about a replacement striker and how they should reassign the field positions. The other kids mostly seemed disappointed about the loss of the whipped cream party. Lilly, for once, had nothing to say about anything, even soccer.

For the rest of the day, the whole class fell into a funk. Jenny's own mood plummeted, as well. She felt worse and worse every time she saw how upset Lilly was about having to miss the soccer game because of a speech evaluation. Jenny soon found herself thinking about all the years she had studied with English tutors. Ms. Candy's story had made perfect sense. When she was first learning English, Jenny had definitely felt like a new lamb learning to walk. Only recently, after many falls and much trying-again, had she begun to feel more confident.

Jenny had never shared Lilly's issue with saying the word 'like' too much. Her big problem with English had been articles of speech, which wasn't all that uncommon for Asian speakers since they don't even exist in their native languages. Jenny felt like she had cried tears for the entire country of China over three words: "a," "an," and "the." Jenny's English tutor would ask her to say a simple sentence such as, "I am going to the store." But, Jenny would repeat it back as, "I am going to store." Leaving out "the" was a constant source of frustration for both student and tutor.

The most recent English tutor was so fed up with reminding Jenny about articles of speech that during their last session he had stormed out of the room, leaving her alone until her mother picked her up an hour later. Jenny hated that tutor with all her heart until she received an English grammar book from him in the mail a few days later. The enclosed note read: "DEAR JENNY, I RE-

MINDED YOU A HUNDRED TIMES ABOUT THE ARTICLES OF SPEECH AND YOU STILL DIDN'T LEARN. LOOK THEM UP YOURSELF AND MAYBE YOU WILL."

Jenny carried the English grammar book with her everywhere. She followed her former tutor's advice and started looking up correct articles of speech until she was speaking better. Jenny finally learned not because some tutor corrected her, but because she had to correct herself. Jenny thought about how much Lilly was suffering. She decided that she was going to help Lilly stop saying "like" just as her former English tutor had taught her how to learn the dreaded articles of speech. Jenny wasn't sure how to do this yet. All she knew was that she needed to act fast because time was running out. Lilly couldn't miss the soccer game.

The rest of the day was largely uneventful. Ms. Candy must have noticed the class' glum mood because she cancelled the afternoon's scheduled activities in favor of a trip to the school library to pick out books for silent reading time. Jenny chose a non-fiction title about spies, hoping to get some ideas about secretly helping Lilly.

As soon as Jenny got home, she raced up to her room to finish reading the new library book, paying special attention to an entire chapter devoted to handwriting disguise. When she was done, Jenny tore out pieces of paper from every type of notebook she owned. Next, she searched for different colored pencils and pens. Then, she spent almost two hours straight writing notes for Ms. Candy's class suggestion box.

Although every one contained the same suggestion, the notes were supposed to be from different students. To make them authentic-looking, Jenny tried to produce every possible combination. One note was written on blue paper with a black pen in all capital letters. Another was written on lined white paper in cursive using a pencil. Yet another was written on sparkly paper with a red pen and included lots of hearts and stars and peace signs. Jenny wrote notes in messy handwriting and notes in neat handwriting. She wrote notes using her natural right hand, her awkward left hand and even with her mouth. She had tried using her toes, too, but not one letter came out clearly. Jenny even typed a note on her computer and printed it out.

Jenny was so quiet that her mother didn't come into her room until it was dinnertime. When her mother noticed the thick book, papers, pens and pencils covering Jenny's bed, she smiled and said, "Wow. Lots of homework."

As Jenny finished her twenty-fourth note she said, "Yes, mommy."

"Good," said her mother and Jenny followed her down to the kitchen.

After dinner, Jenny went right back up to her room. She spent another two hours writing, but this time it wasn't homework or even note-writing. Even though she was exhausted, Jenny put on her earphones and surrendered to her comic book until she fell fast asleep.

Friday, February 5:
Exploding Emotions

Room 147 was still dark when Jenny arrived. With the lights off, everything appeared gloomy, grey and eerily lifeless, more like a haunted house instead of an elementary school classroom. The stacked chairs on the top of the desks looked like guard dogs standing at attention. Jenny shuddered as she stepped inside, frightened that somehow, they were watching her every move. She pulled her jacket close and when the papers stuffed inside made a crinkling noise, she gasped. As she scanned the classroom, Jenny's heart thumped as loudly as a drum and only when she was certain that she was alone, did she start to breathe again. On the way toward Ms. Candy's desk, Jenny noticed Lilly's soccer sweatshirt in her cubby, and she was reminded that helping someone was worth the risk of getting caught.

After last night's "homework" extravaganza, Jenny's mother had prepared her specialty, deep-fried Chinese cruller donuts, for breakfast, a meal that she typically reserved only for visiting relatives. And when Jenny had asked to leave for school thirty minutes early for extra study time, her mother had practically jumped for joy, smiling with a face full of pride, a face Jenny hadn't seen in a very long time. As she took a bite of her hot cruller, Jenny hoped that her new-found love for school didn't seem too suspicious.

A wave of nausea rolled across her stomach and immediately, Jenny regretted eating so many crullers at breakfast. Dread and donuts were turning out to be a horrible mix. When she reached Ms. Candy's desk, Jenny pulled out the stack of notes she had smuggled in her jacket. She began stuffing them into the suggestion box as quickly as she could. When a few unexpected problems with the box's small opening slowed her down, Jenny began to sweat. Now, in addition to reeking of suspicion, she just plain reeked. As she dropped in the last note, Jenny heard a noise. Frozen like a statue, she listened while someone unzipped a bag in the fifth-grade office. Jenny grabbed her backpack and darted toward the door, making it out just as Mr. Short peered around the corner.

In the bathroom stall sitting with her feet on the toilet lid, Jenny caught her breath, relieved to get all the notes into the suggestion box without anyone noticing. The sound of the students arriving in the hallways signaled the start of the school day and just as Jenny was about to get down off the toilet, she heard a girl come into the bathroom and begin to cry. After a few minutes, she heard the girl wash her face and then roll out paper towels to dry it. As the girl started to leave, Jenny stretched her head toward the bottom of the stall door and watched a pair of baby pink shoes walk away.

No one noticed Jenny slinking into her chair at the end of morning arrival. Yesterday's damp mood had disappeared and the students, including Lilly, were loud and busy again. To Jenny, the whole atmosphere of the classroom seemed bright and cheerful, and not just because the lights had been turned on, but because of her teacher. Ms. Candy was floating around in a dress made entirely of dictionary pages. Small strips of paper had been woven together to form the top and the bottom contained two puffy layers full of pages. For a belt, Ms. Candy had sewn on a thick piece of green felt that was decorated with the words "REDUCE, REUSE, RECYCLE, RESPELL!" A sparkly silver tiara sat on the top of her blonde hair, which was styled into a bun.

"Morning Meeting!" Ms. Candy called and the class scrambled to take their places on the rug. As Nadia sat down in the front, Ms. Candy smiled at her and said, "You're back! And, don't you look prettier than a glob of butter melting on a stack of pancakes!"

Nadia smoothed her dress. "My dad got it for me after my other dress was ruined by whomever wrote on the rulers with black marker," she said. In the back, Aidan fidgeted with his shirt.

"Speaking of pretty things," Ms. Candy said, "Mr. Short found a beautiful silk hair bow on our floor this morning." Holding up a purple bow with gold flowers, Ms. Candy asked, "Does this look familiar?" The girls studied the bow with intensity. "Maybe someone who was in class on the earlier side of arrival since it was found when Mr. Short first came in?" Jenny, who almost always wore braids with bows made of Chinese silk, felt her hair and realized that the left one was missing. As quickly and quietly as she had stuffed the notes into the suggestion box, Jenny ripped out the right bow and stuffed it into her pocket. "No takers?" asked Ms. Candy. The entire class, including Jenny, shook their heads. "Well, I'll keep it safe and sound until someone claims it."

"And, you've probably noticed my new dress!" said Ms. Candy as she twirled around. "My neighbor was planning to throw out her old dictionary and I thought, 'Why not reuse it?' One person's trash is another person's treasure! So, I tore out the pages and sewed 'em together, paired it with a tiara and—voila—The Spelling Queen!" The class applauded while Ms. Candy twirled around. Ms. Candy said, "And now, my royal subjects, let us begin today's first activity, a surprise spelling test!" Some students began to grumble but most of them started to smile when Ms. Candy said, "I order you to have fun!" Jenny was thinking about how difficult it was not to smile around Ms. Candy, when Nadia stood up in front of her.

"My dad bought me new shoes, too, Ms. Candy," Nadia bragged.

"Very fancy!" Ms. Candy said as she walked toward the front of the room holding the spelling word list. Jenny was admiring them, too, when she remembered where she had seen them before—on the girl who was crying in the bathroom. Then, she thought about the purple bow in her pocket and all the fake notes in the suggestion box. Jenny sat down and studied Nadia, and felt both comforted and disheartened by the awareness that she wasn't the only one with secrets.

Just like she promised, Ms. Candy did manage to make the spelling test fun. In addition to using silly accents to exaggerate each word's syllables, she danced around the classroom in her Spelling Queen outfit, acting out the definition. Even Aidan looked amused, particularly when she used his cheeks as an example for "freckle." To explain "adroit" Lilly pretended to score a goal on Ms. Candy. Nadia modeled her new clothes for "immaculate." Tanner's hair had been a clue for "shaggy."

Ms. Candy brought in Mr. Short to explain three words. "Teacher" was obvious to everyone. For "confrontation," she pretended to have an argument with him but instead of yelling back, Mr. Short stood still looking uncomfortable. For "snuggle," Ms. Candy dramatically cuddled and hugged Mr. Short until the class began to giggle and make kissing noises. When Mr. Short walked back to his classroom, both teachers were blushing.

After Ms. Candy had a coughing fit and pretended to faint for the last word, "suffering," the class passed up their spelling tests to the front of the room. Ms. Candy shuffled the papers and handed them back out. She provided the correct spellings as the students graded each other. This was supposed to be done in confidence, but Tyler shouted out, "Perfect score for Nadia!" in front of the entire class. No one seemed surprised, especially Nadia.

When Jenny got her own test back, she did as well as she predicted, badly. Although Ms. Candy had been fun to watch, Jenny had trouble understanding her southern accent, and more than half of the words were spelled incorrectly. Frowning, Jenny started to fold her test in half to hide her score when she noticed that a note with the words "TO: JEN-

NY" had been placed on her desk. Jenny looked around for the sender, but everyone seemed to be listening to Ms. Candy discuss the details of next week's spelling bee. Wrapping the note inside her test, she opened it up and pretended to put the papers in her drawer. Not only did the handwriting look the same as the note from her first day, but the message was identical. "IT'S ALL GOOD."

Jenny remembered that she had received the first note after her terrible math quiz performance, which made her wonder if the sender had also seen her terrible spelling test score. Before she lined up for recess, Jenny glanced at the note one more time before putting it next to the purple hair bow in her pocket. Haverswell Elementary wasn't necessarily "all good," but the secret notes had made Jenny feel a little better about fitting in with totally unfamiliar people and places.

Outside, the class was practicing for the Fifth-Grade Soccer Game. With Lilly on the sidelines, Tyler was without a scoring partner and had been unable to connect any passes with the new strikers. The entire offensive and defensive lineups had been changed and many of the students weren't exactly sure what position they were supposed to play, which resulted in chaos on the field. When Jack completely missed a kick and fell over, Coach Adkins had shaken his head in frustration and declared that the class "looked like chickens running around with their heads cut off." Once she translated the words back into Chinese, the image had made Jenny laugh out loud. Southern sayings were quickly becoming one of her favorite things about leaving California.

However frenzied she may have appeared, Jenny was enjoying herself and feeling a little more comfortable with soccer. She ran and ran without tiring, enjoying being able to pass back and move the ball down the field without having to say a word. Coach Adkins had just called five minutes remaining in the game when a ball came barreling toward Jenny, who was standing in the penalty box.

Jenny looked around for someone to pass it to, but she soon realized that she was, in fact, the most forward person on the field. Tyler and Coach Adkins yelled, "Shoot! Shoot!" With the pressure of everyone staring at her, Jenny began to panic. The opposing team's players were running toward her from both directions and the goalie looked like a tiger ready to pounce. "Shoot!" Tyler yelled again, but Jenny just froze.

And then, out of nowhere, Tanner appeared next to Jenny. His long bangs flopped up and down as he nodded encouragingly. Jenny smiled back, then closed her eyes and swung her foot at the ball. She didn't hit the ball hard, but she did aim it precisely toward the top corner. The goalkeeper reached for the ball, but he couldn't make contact, and it trickled into the goal. With her team cheering behind her and Tanner continuing to flash his big-braces smile, Jenny jumped up and down in celebration, full of happiness. She couldn't believe she had scored! She didn't want the moment to end. Ever.

But it did, when Jenny realized, in what felt like slow motion, that both the her purple hair bow and the secret note had fallen out of her pocket, and landed on the field in front of her. While everyone continued to applaud, Jenny grabbed her bow before anyone recognized it as the match to the one Mr. Short had found earlier. At the same time, Tanner picked up the note and handed it to Jenny with a smile that she didn't think could get much bigger. The mishmash of emotions was way too much for Jenny's stomach to handle. Clutching her sides, she crammed the bow and note into her pocket, and sprinted off the field toward the bathroom.

In the bathroom Jenny waited for the nausea to pass. The secret note was now shredded and buried in the trash can. As Jenny tried to figure out if she should get rid of the hair bow, too, Nadia walked in with black marker covering her fingers. Jenny must have been staring because as Nadia began to wash her hands she said matter-of-factly, "I was helping in the front office during soccer practice." She scrubbed furiously and said, "There's no way I'm ruining another dress!" Nadia dried off and threw the paper towels into the trash. Jenny hoped she wouldn't notice the torn-up note. Turning to leave, Nadia looked at Jenny's hands and said, "By the way, pretty bow." Jenny gasped. The purple hair bow, displayed like a prized possession, was still in her hand.

At lunch an hour later, Jenny still felt sick. The leftover cruller in her lunch box had almost required another bathroom visit. Sipping slowly from her water bottle, Jenny was trying to drown out the cafeteria noise when Aidan's lunch tray collided with the table. Jenny looked up and Aidan mumbled, "Can I sit here?" Aidan had asked the same question for the past two days, and both times Jenny had shrugged her shoulders just like she did today. "Well, if you don't tell me that I can't, then I'm—," he started. But instead of finishing the warning this time, Aidan plopped down three seats away. As he drenched his french fries in vinegar and salt, he said, "I mean, great goal today," which caused Jenny to blush and Mr. Short to glance their way.

No one spoke for the rest of lunch until Aidan came back from clearing his tray. Showing off a handful of vinegar and salt packets, he announced excitedly, "Double french fry day for me! We're having them for dinner, too!" Mr. Short, who was busy squirting gooey cupcake filling into his mouth, hardly looked over. Although the mere mention of food, especially greasy American favorites, made her stomach upset, Jenny tried her best to smile.

The first thing Ms. Candy did after lunch was walk over to her desk and pick up the suggestion box. As she presented it to the class, Tyler shouted, "Dude, look how full it is!"

Ms. Candy nodded her head in agreement and said, "Someone's been very busy thinking about how we can improve our class! When I came in this morning, the suggestion box was stuffed!" Jenny gulped. "I'll take a look at them over the weekend, y'all," Ms. Candy said. Looking firmly at Aidan, she continued, "I just hope they aren't some of the silly ideas we've had in the past."

Aidan sighed defiantly and getting up from his chair he said, "I forgot to wash my hands."

While Aidan was at the sink cleaning up, Ms. Candy moved on to a math exercise about graphing. Each person would tell the class their favorite color. After the responses were tallied, the class would make bar graphs, line graphs and pie charts with the data. Ms. Candy explained that in addition to teaching them about math, she hoped the color information would provide ideas about how to personalize their valentines. Because she couldn't wait to start on her cards, Jenny listened intently to everyone's responses, so much so that she didn't realize when it was her turn to answer.

"How about you, Jenny? What's your favorite color?" Ms. Candy asked. Jenny had not said one word since she arrived that Monday. Her face heated up as she began to speak.

"P...," Jenny tried softly.

"Pink?" offered Tyler.

"P...," Jenny began as her nausea surfaced again.

"Purple!" yelled Lilly.

"Peach?" asked Nadia.

"Powder blue!" Jack said.

Ms. Candy shook her head and said, "Give Jenny a chance to answer, y'all!"

Jenny took a deep breath and said, "Puce." But no one heard her answer, and this time it wasn't because of her quiet voice. At the exact moment that Jenny had opened her mouth to speak, Aidan exploded a volcano in the sink.

Ms. Candy and Nadia screamed. Many students, including Lilly and Tanner, were sprayed with water. Tyler and Jack began to hoot and holler. As bubbles sprang up from the volcano and onto the floor, Aidan didn't even try to hide his culpability. A can of baking soda and soap from the supply closet, and the now-empty vinegar and salt packets he had taken from the cafeteria littered the counters. Plus, Aidan's laughs were louder than anything else in the room.

Pandemonium that rivaled the volcano's haphazard blasts filled the classroom. When Mr. Short arrived, Ms. Candy was attempting to mop up the bubbles from the floor with a sponge. Mr. Short did not comment on the volcano or the bubbles or even the fact that some of the students were crying because they were sopping wet. He just looked sadly at Ms. Candy's Spelling Queen costume and sighed, "Your beautiful dress!"

Ms. Candy's new outfit now appeared like it had been left out in a hurricane. The top ruffle had wilted into the bottom one and most of the dictionary pages had begun to tear. As she wiped a mix of tears and volcano water from her eyes, Ms. Candy slipped on some of the bubbles. She cried, "Would one of y'all bring me the broom and help me sweep up before I literally and figuratively fly off the handle?"

Tyler and Nadia raced toward the supply closet. Nadia tried to push past him, but Tyler was faster and Nadia's new shoes caused her to stumble across the floor. As Tyler took out the broom Nadia shouted, "I wanted to get it!"

"What the—!" Tyler yelled. He held up the broom so that everyone could see that it was covered with black marker. When Ms. Candy shook her head in disbelief her tiara went flying off her head and landed in the trash can.

"Aidan!" Ms. Candy shouted.

Aidan sheepishly approached and said, "Ms. Candy, I made the volcano but I didn't write on the—"

Ms. Candy motioned for Mr. Short to come over. She whispered, "I'm as mad as a donkey chewing on bumblebees! Do you mind dealing with Aidan?" Mr. Short nodded. As he led Aidan out of the room Ms. Candy added in a voice that everyone could hear,

"And, Mr. Short, on your way to Principal Brimstone's office, would you please remind Aidan that destroying school property will result in a suspension?"

Jenny was already ready for the weekend to begin when her mother dropped her off at the piano studio after school. If she could make it through meeting her new piano teacher and an hour-long lesson, then she would be able to spend the weekend in her room listening to music, drawing in her note-book and making valentines. The last five days had been busy and noisy and chaotic and exciting and difficult and fun. Jenny was used to change, but so much all at once had exhausted her. She needed a quiet weekend to relax.

The first thing that Mrs. Sheldon, her pi-ano teacher, did after introducing herself was to hand Jenny a sheet of music and an-nounce, "We're having a little Valentine's Day recital next Sunday and I'd like you to play!" Jenny quickly did the math. Two Sundays from today would give her exactly nine days to practice. Mrs. Sheldon said apologetically, "I know this piece is much too easy for you, but with such short notice it's all I could come up with!"

Even with months of practice, Jenny knew that she could never learn how to play the piece, and that it was actually much too hard for her. But, she didn't admit any of this to Mrs. Sheldon. She simply smiled politely and began to play her scales.

In the waiting room after her lesson, Jenny reached into her backpack and pulled out her notebook. Although her mother would be arriving soon, she needed to write. Jenny figured that two minutes was better than nothing.

Saturday, February 6:
The Four Situations

The first time that Jenny woke up it was just before seven o'clock in the morning. When she realized that she hadn't actually missed her alarm, Jenny was relieved, and rolled over to cuddle her soft teddy bear. The past five days had been stressful, the first week at a new school always was, and she was happy to have the weekend to relax. A smile spread across Jenny's face as she thought dreamily about the Secret Note Writer. "It's all good," she said to herself, pulling the covers over her head. Instantly, she fell back asleep.

Two hours later, Jenny woke up again. This time, she was gasping for breath after having been trapped in a nightmare in which the new piano teacher, Mrs. Sheldon, had given her an extremely difficult piece to learn by the Valentine's Day Recital. In the dream, Jenny tried to explain that the piece was too hard, but Mrs. Sheldon just wouldn't listen. Over and over, Jenny had shouted, "I can't! I can't!" But, the words wouldn't come out, not even a whisper.

And then suddenly, Jenny was at the recital, sweating under the stage's bright lights, aware of the keys beneath her fingers but afraid to press them, afraid to make a mistake. Then just as suddenly, she slipped off the piano bench onto the floor. As she searched the audience for someone to help, from the first row her mother shouted, "Jenny, get up! Jenny, get up!"

But now, in addition to being unable to speak, Jenny couldn't move. Lying on the stage floor, she struggled to pull herself up and to scream, "I can't! I can't!" As her desperation grew and grew, Jenny noticed her mother walking toward her with a bucket of water, shaking her head in disappointment. Paralyzed, Jenny shut her eyes. She knew what was coming next.

When she finally opened her eyes, Jenny saw that her mother was standing above her, pressing a cool washcloth onto her forehead. "Jenny, get up! Jenny, get up!" her mother said. With each deep breath, Jenny woke up more and more. Only when she was fully awake after her mother had pulled away the covers that had been entangling her, did Jenny understand that she was not on stage. Relieved to be back in her own bedroom, Jenny took another deep breath. In a voice made hoarse from trying to scream, she said, "I'm up, Mommy."

"Breakfast," said Jenny's mother.

As her mother walked out of the room, Jenny sat up and replied, "Okay. I'm coming."

A fried cooking smell drifted up from the kitchen. Jenny hoped that her mother hadn't made crullers again. Even though she had brushed her teeth at least five times before

bed last night, her mouth still tasted like yesterday's breakfast. Just thinking about the
hot donuts made her queasy, and as she put
on her robe and slippers, she stumbled a little
toward the bench of her electronic piano,
knocking the sheet music to the floor. Jenny
looked down at the piece Mrs. Sheldon had
assigned her to play at the recital and sighed.
The music was still difficult, she still couldn't
learn it in nine days and she still hadn't told
her piano teacher the truth about her piano
skills.

Thankfully, breakfast was back to normal,
a bowl of fresh fruit and a piece of whole
wheat toast with fried eggs. Downstairs was
so quiet that she actually heard her orange
slice squirt open when she took a bite. As
Jenny ate, her mother drank pot after pot of
tea in the living room while making her way
through a stack of week-old *China Daily*
newspapers that Jenny's father had brought
home from wherever he had been traveling to
that week. Before heading off to the golf
course for the rest of the day, Jenny's father
had made his typical Saturday morning ap-

pearance, asking quickly about her new school and then giving her a bag of her favorite Chinese taffy.

Back in her room, Jenny chewed taffy and tried to learn the piano piece, but she could barely make it past the introduction of the first movement before her fingers and eyes and ears stopped talking to each other. Her heart wasn't in it, either. Sometimes, when Jenny was upset, playing piano actually made her feel better. All of the sadness flowed through her body and then was released like drops of rain from a storm cloud, out through her fingertips and onto the keys. But, she wasn't sad about the piano recital. She was worried. It was her nightmare come true.

The difficult piano piece stared back at her and all she wanted to do was rip it to shreds like Tyler did to the stickers. How she would ever be able to admit to her teacher and her mother that she didn't know how to play it, remained a mystery. "Who ever heard of a piano recital on Valentine's Day, anyway?" Jenny snickered to herself. "Not that I'll get any valentine cards," she sighed, doubting if anyone in her class besides Ms. Candy even knew her name yet.

"I should be the one to talk," Jenny thought. "I don't know much, either." Once she started, she couldn't help but create a list in her head of all the things she hadn't been able to do in her first week at Haverswell Elementary: play difficult piano pieces, multiply, spell, speak in front of people or understand southern accents. Sighing, she asked herself if she really knew anything, any one thing worth knowing. As the answer came to her, Jenny's head slumped onto the piano keys in defeat and she began to cry.

When Jenny lifted her head a moment later, it wasn't because she suddenly felt better about everything; she simply wanted another piece of taffy. As she bit into the candy, the vanilla flavoring filled her mouth and she thought, "It's all good." And then, perhaps because she was exhausted from a crazy week or tired of trying to learn the piano piece or maybe because the Secret Note Writer's message finally made sense, Jenny fell off the piano bench, just like in her nightmare. This time, however, she wasn't paralyzed on the ground, crying out for help. Instead, Jenny laughed hysterically until her stomach hurt.

"It's all good!" Jenny laughed out loud as she realized that at least one other person besides Ms. Candy did, in fact, know her name. The Secret Note Writer had written it out, twice. And then, Jenny began to remember all the things that she did know. Jenny knew that she was the only person besides Nadia to easily learn the words to the South Carolina song. "It's all good!" Jenny said again. She was laughing so hard that tears poured down her face. Jenny thought about how much her soccer skills had improved in a week. "I even scored a goal!" she cheered. When she finally stopped laughing, Jenny got up from the floor, plopped onto her bed and nestled into her pillow. She leafed through the pages of her notebook, pleased with how much progress she had made on her new comic. Everything that was going on in school, home and piano lessons had actually given her tons of inspiration. Then, Jenny thought about how much secret progress she had made on solving her three class problems.

First, there was the situation with Ms. Candy and Mr. Short. From all Ms. Candy's sweet talk, Jenny was sure that she was in love with Mr. Short. And, she knew he felt the same way, always looking at her like she was the most special candy in the box. Jenny chuckled. On the surface, Ms. Candy and Mr. Short seemed like total opposites. Ms. Candy was vivacious and artistic and fun. Among all the different places she had lived and in all the schools she had attended, Ms. Candy was the most unique teacher Jenny had ever met. Mr. Short, on the other hand, was quiet and a little boring. If Ms. Candy was a rainbow-striped zebra in a parade, then Mr. Short was a chameleon that blended in with his sur-roundings.

Jenny had also noticed, however, that both teachers had a lot of things in common, starting with all the blushing and winking that went on between them. Because Jenny was quiet herself, she knew that there was a lot of meaning in the way your body talked. Your smile could show how much you loved something or a wink of an eye could mean something secret. Jenny remembered how Ms. Candy had snuggled with Mr. Short during the spelling test and how Mr. Short had saved Ms. Candy from crashing into the wall during Aidan's water fountain prank. They were both very sweet, Jenny thought, especially with each other.

In addition to acting sweet, Jenny knew for certain that both teachers loved to eat sweets, a lot, although they hadn't yet admitted this to each other. Jenny had already caught Ms. Candy sneaking pizza cookie cake and a frosted donut, and Mr. Short never mentioned his daily vending machine cupcakes. What was keeping them from being boyfriend-girlfriend, Jenny believed, was maybe nothing more than their sweet tooth secrets. As she opened up another taffy, Jenny wondered how she could help Ms. Candy and Mr. Short discover the truth about each other's love of sweets and of each other. Jenny didn't know how she was going to do this, but as she looked down at the giant heart she had sketched in her notebook, she was sure about one thing—Valentine's Day would provide the perfect opportunity.

Second, there was the situation with another pair of opposites, Nadia and Aidan. Unlike Ms. Candy and Mr. Short, however, Jenny didn't think her classmates had anything in common, except that they were both good at annoying people, especially each other. They were also good at intimidating Jenny. Aidan looked like a cuddly teddy bear up until the point that he got irritated. Jenny was scared of his unpredictable moodiness and prayed that she would never be the target of one of his pranks. Nadia looked and acted like a confident high-society house cat, dressing in perfectly coordinated outfits that she didn't like to get dirty. But, Nadia was also quick to react when she felt threatened.

Already, Jenny had been the target of Nadia's intense stare and her nasty tone. Both had stung like a cat scratch.

At the beginning of the week, Jenny was convinced that Aidan was ruining the school supplies. It wasn't that big of a stretch to assume that the person who booby traps chairs with stickers or rigs water fountains or puts food dye in soap dispensers or explodes volcanoes in the sink—Aidan—was the same person who would destroy school property. Nadia, herself, always seemed quick to point the finger at him in front of the class. Even Ms. Candy, who Jenny believed to be extremely fair and understanding, seemed to arrive at the same conclusion.

By Wednesday, Jenny wasn't so sure Aidan was guilty. Although Aidan admitted blame for the pranks, Jenny had noticed that he always insisted that he hadn't touched the school supplies. With each occurrence, Aidan's protests had increased. For someone who got in trouble so often, Jenny thought it was strange to be upset about what was seemingly just a drop in a barrel of mischief.

To Jenny, Nadia had seemed like the perfect teacher's pet until she claimed that the marker from the rulers had ruined her dress, which Jenny knew wasn't true. Nadia had stood next to her earlier, at music class, and tried to hide the black smudges. Jenny also thought it was revealing that no school property had been destroyed on the day Nadia was absent. When Nadia was at school, she always had an excuse to leave Ms. Candy and the students when they were at an activity outside the classroom. Nadia claimed that she needed to take care of an injury or to help in the office, but Jenny believed the excuses were instead, perfect opportunities to destroy school property without anyone knowing.

What had given Nadia away more than anything, though, were the black marks that often covered her fingers. Jenny thought it was odd that a girl who seemed the exact opposite of dirty would allow her hands to be filthy. Plus, because Jenny worked on her comics every day, she knew exactly how your fingers turned black, by writing with a black marker. By the time she left school yesterday,

Jenny was positive that Aidan was innocent and Nadia was guilty. But at the rate he was going, Jenny was sure that Aidan would be suspended from school very soon for destroying the supplies before anyone discovered the truth.

Third, there was the situation with Lilly. Jenny hoped that her plan to help Lilly stop saying the word "like" too much would work. As she pictured Ms. Candy reading through all the fake notes she had put in the suggestion box, Jenny felt a twinge of excitement—her plan was in motion. Jenny figured that she would find out what Ms. Candy would do when she got to school on Monday. One thing was certain, however; Lilly had to be at the Fifth-Grade Soccer Game instead of at a speech evaluation. The class weren't going to win the game or the whipped cream party without her.

All the ideas about how to help Ms. Candy and Mr. Short, Aidan and Nadia, and Lilly, swirled around in Jenny's head. But instead of making her feel overwhelmed, trying to solve the three situations thrilled Jenny. It was one more thing she felt happy about knowing how to do well. That was, until Jenny glanced over at her piano and wondered if this secret talent would help solve her own giant problem, too. Jenny just couldn't handle thinking about the Valentine's Day Recital anymore. What she needed right now was to get all the emotions, good and bad, out.

The library book about spies caught Jenny's eye when she reached for her notebook. Giggling with anticipation, she opened to the chapter called, "How to Make a Quick Exit." Unable to believe her luck, Jenny shook her head; she had remembered correctly. The solution, a long list of ways to fake getting sick, was right in front of her. Jenny quickly decided which trick to try out first.

"Mommy, Mommy!" yelled Jenny.

Jenny's mother, who was unaccustomed to hearing her daughter shout or ask for help, ran upstairs. Halfway up, her silk slippers caused her to lose her footing and she tripped back down a few stairs before starting up again. Completely out of breath, Jenny's mother pushed open the door and hobbled into the room. "Jenny!" she panted.

With Nadia's dramatic flair in mind, Jenny pretended to be as sick as possible, letting out a little whimper and stretching her face toward her mother for a thorough examination. Although her face was red and blotchy like she had intended, all the pinching and skin twisting had also created lots of white nail marks. Each cheek looked like a scoop of strawberry ice cream topped with vanilla sprinkles. "You drink milk at school?" her mother asked.

Instantly annoyed that her mother didn't fall for the scam—she hadn't even suggested the possibility of looking flushed—Jenny dropped the sick act. She thought of what the worst troublemaker she knew, Aidan, would do if he found himself caught in a lie he didn't want to explain. When Jenny shrugged her shoulders, her mother's eyes opened widely, full of shock. Even when she was a little girl, Jenny had never purposely ignored anyone, especially her mother. "You drink milk at school?" her mother repeated.

One act of rebellion today was enough for Jenny to handle. Defeated, she fell back onto her bed and answered, "No, Mommy."

Jenny's mother took a deep breath. "Come down. I make tea," she said. Jenny nodded. "And, I get ice for foot," she added with the slightest bit of annoyance as she limped out of the bedroom.

As soon as her mother left, Jenny jumped out of bed and surveyed her face in the mirror. "She's right, I don't look sick," Jenny sighed. "I look ridiculous." Taking out her notebook, Jenny stretched out on her bed. She had ten minutes to work on her story while the tea brewed.

SUNDAY, FEBRUARY 7:
OVERHEATED

After church, Jenny's family attended a pot-luck at Eddie Wang's house. While the adults marveled at her mother's specialty, deep-fried Chinese crullers, Jenny and Eddie talked about school. Eddie was happy when he found out that she was in Ms. Candy's class. In his southern accent, he described Ms. Candy as "the best teacher ever" and, as both "awesome" and "totally cool." When Eddie left to play video games with the other boys, Jenny fixed a plate of food and then squeezed between one of the Wang's lazy cats and Eddie's sleeping grandmother on the couch. Surrounded by purrs and snores, Jenny picked at her food and thought about what Ms. Candy had done at school following the exploding volcano incident. She agreed with Eddie about Ms. Candy being awesome and totally cool, but to Jenny, she was also just like her mother's crullers—special.

Ms. Candy had been determined to finish the math activity and as soon as the classroom was cleaned up, she began to ask everyone about their favorite color. "Jenny," she said cheerfully, "I do believe it was your turn."

"Puce," said Jenny.

"Puke?" asked Tyler. Immediately, the class broke out in laughter.

"Puce," Jenny whispered, her face reddened with embarrassment.

"Your favorite color is like, vomit?" asked Lilly.

Although she was mortified that no one had a clue what color she was talking about, Jenny was relieved about one thing, that Mr. Short had taken Aidan to the principal's office. Aidan would have delighted in pointing out all the disgusting details, which would have made the situation much more difficult for her to stomach. With the class clown, the gross-out possibilities were endless.

"Puce," Jenny said again.

"Dude, I think I'm going to gag!" Jack moaned.

"Enough," said Ms. Candy, shaking her head. "Jenny, can you repeat that a little louder, sugar."

Remembering the often-repeated advice of her English tutors, Jenny sat up straight and took a deep breath. "Puce," she said, in her loudest and most confident voice.

"PUCE!" exclaimed Ms. Candy. "Well, doesn't that just take the cake? Puce was the color of my evening gown when I won the Miss South Carolina pageant!" Ms. Candy clapped her hands giddily, which squelched any remaining laughter. "Five layers of chiffon ruffles sprinkled with diamonds!"

Jack still looked confused. "Puke?" he asked again.

"No, puce. P-U-C-E," Ms. Candy explained.

"Never heard of it," said Tyler.

"It's a shade of pink, kind of like the color of my new shoes," Nadia said with conviction, kicking them to the side of her chair for everyone to see.

"Actually, Nadia," Ms. Candy gently corrected, "puce isn't pink, but more of a brownish-purple color." Jenny studied Ms. Candy as she danced around the room. Although the water from Aidan's volcano had destroyed her teacher's Spelling Queen outfit, it definitely had not dampened an ounce of her spirit. "Let's just say you wouldn't find puce in a pack of crayons!" Ms. Candy said. "Puce is pretty unique."

Jenny wanted to yell out, "Just like you, Ms. Candy!" As if Ms. Candy could read Jenny's thoughts, she smiled back.

Ms. Candy squeezed Jenny's shoulders affectionately and said, "Puce is my favorite color, too!" Jenny tingled with the excitement of knowing that they both loved the same thing, something that no one else had even heard about. For once, being unusual hadn't made Jenny weird, it had made her "awesome" and "totally cool," just like Ms. Candy. For a brief, perfect moment, Jenny understood how Ms. Candy must feel all the time.

Sprawled out on her bed after the potluck, Jenny surrounded herself with art supplies. Markers, crayons, paper, stamps, glue, and colored pencils, were the things that made her feel at home in whatever city she was living in. For as long as she could remember, all Jenny wanted to do was create things.

The process was so simultaneously exciting and calming that hours would pass without Jenny even stopping to realize it. If math or spelling or piano was a struggle, than working on art projects was like a leisurely trip down the most-refreshing-shade-of-blue river; or like laying in a flower-covered meadow with nothing to do but soak up the yellow-orange sunshine; or like free-falling into the puffiest white cloud ever. To Jenny, art was absolute joy.

Jenny also liked art because through her projects, she was able to say the things she really wanted to say but didn't, because she was either too shy or couldn't find the right words. Making valentines for the exchange was a chance for Jenny to tell her new class how she felt about them without having to say a word. Even more appealing, was the fact that she wouldn't even have to sign her name on the cards.

After reading down the list of favorite colors from the graphing exercise, Jenny matched up the right paper color with each person. Then, she thought about how to customize each valentine. Lilly's card would be a testament to her awesome soccer skills and Tyler's, to his love of Carolina football. Nadia's card would be pink and fancy to reflect her sense of style, while Aidan's would be filled with soft materials, just like Jenny imagined him to be when he wasn't getting in trouble. Jack's card would be comical and Tanner's would be shiny, just like his all-braces smile. Jenny picked up her drawing pencil. She couldn't wait to start.

Two hours later, as Jenny was decorating Lilly's valentine with soccer balls in the same colors as her coordinated soccer outfits, her mother called, "Jenny?"

"Yes, Mommy?" Jenny answered.

"You practice piano," said her mother from the bottom of the stairs.

"I'm doing homework, Mommy," reasoned Jenny, even though she knew that her mother would not relent until she heard music and that she, herself, would not push her mother much further.

"Drawing not homework," Jenny's mother said. "Recital in one week."

"Yes, Mommy," Jenny sighed. Reluctantly, Jenny scooted off her bed and onto the electronic piano bench.

Lessons with music teachers required Jenny's full concentration, especially since playing was not something that came easily or that she enjoyed all that much. Within a fraction of a second, Jenny not only had to decide whether the notes she read were correct, but she had to get her fingers to press the corresponding keys for the right amount of time. Jenny also had to know when and which foot pedal to step down on, in order to produce the right tone.

Practice at home was different. If her mother wasn't lurking nearby, Jenny was able to let her mind wander a bit more, especially during her scale warm-up. Without even having to think, one side of her brain played notes in a memorized order over and over. Although Jenny detested playing scales because they were so boring, she also appreciated that their simplicity allowed the other side of her brain to daydream. Some of her best comic book ideas had actually developed during scale practice, when her brain was doing two very different things at once.

Today, however, Jenny's daydreams had nothing to do with her comic book. They were all about how she could get out of the piano recital. Recalling the "fake red-face" incident from yesterday annoyed Jenny, mostly because she had failed to do anything except look silly. As Jenny played the ascending D minor scale, a scale she had played hundreds of times, she wondered if it was worthwhile to try another trick from the spy book. In the five second pause before starting the descending scale, she decided that it was far less embarrassing to mess up a trick at home in front of her mother than to mess up on stage in front of an entire audience who had been told that she was a piano superstar.

Minutes later, Jenny was holding the spy book in her left hand while she continued to play scales with her right hand. Among the list of tricks, one stood out to Jenny that seemed pretty easy to pull off—faking a high temperature. In eleven years, Jenny had not been sick very often. The worst time was in second grade when an infection in both ears caused her temperature to skyrocket to 105 degrees. Jenny had missed school for over a week. If she could pull off this scam, she would miss the recital. Abruptly, Jenny stopped playing the piano and called out, "Mommy! Mommy!"

Jenny's mother ran up the stairs just as fast as the day before. When she pushed open the door, Jenny was spread out on the bed as if she had suddenly fainted. Every few seconds, little grunts and moans emerged from her wide-open mouth. Her tongue flopped to the side, seemingly immovable, and her left hand was draped dramatically across her head. To avoid any question about the extent to which she was suffering, Jenny's right hand gripped her stomach with theatric flair that would have impressed even Nadia. Jenny's mother surveyed the scene and asked, "What's wrong?" Squeezing her eyes closed, Jenny let out a few loud groans. "You sick?"

When her mother was standing next to the bed she studied her head and said, "Let me feel."

Just like the spy book had instructed, Jenny refused to move her hand. "Let me feel," her mother insisted. The book also warned that this might happen and so again, Jenny followed its instructions, continuing to moan loudly and rocking back and forth to show that the suffering was just too much for her to bear. The book's advice worked like a charm and Jenny couldn't help smiling to herself as her mother backed out of the room and said, "I get thermometer."

A few minutes later, Jenny's mother returned. As she stuck the thermometer into Jenny's mouth, her face revealed a hint of worry. With pursed lips, Jenny held the thermometer in place while she counted in her head. When she got to ten, Jenny unexpectedly jumped off the bed, which caused her mother to scream. Clutching her stomach, Jenny darted into the bathroom with the thermometer hung in her mouth like a pipe, mumbling, "Toilet!"

"You, okay?" Jenny's mother asked worriedly from outside the bathroom door.

In the bathroom, Jenny groaned and made coughing noises while she rolled the end of the thermometer between her thumb and index finger. After a few seconds, she checked the temperature—92 degrees. Jenny panicked. It was way too low. For her mother to think she was sick, she needed to get the reading over 100 degrees. Jenny rubbed the thermometer again, but she got the same result.

"Jenny!" her mother called.

To avoid answering, Jenny continued to groan loudly and then flushed the toilet several times. Recalling the spy book's step-by-step instructions, she tried to figure out what she was doing wrong when it suddenly occurred to her to check the thermometer type. Jenny realized that she was following the electric thermometer plan even though she was using a mercury model. Taking a deep breath, she began again with the right plan.

The hot water had been running for close to two minutes when Jenny's mother yelled, "Come out! Now!"

After a few attempts at dipping the tip of the thermometer into the hot water, the thermometer reading had only reached 99 degrees, which was still too low to indicate any serious illness. Jenny flushed the toilet again and said, "One minute, Mommy!" Aware that her time was running out, Jenny turned off the water and decided to try the book's backup plan, which called for using a light bulb instead of hot water, to increase the temperature. Although it felt like the heat was burning a hole in her fingers, Jenny managed to press the thermometer against the bathroom light for exactly one minute.

Just as her mother opened the door, Jenny popped the thermometer back into her mouth. In order to avoid any drop in temperature, she handed it to her mother as quickly as possible. Her mother studied the results and then she studied Jenny, who was continuing to moan and groan. Without saying a word, Jenny's mother passed back the thermometer. The temperature read 118 degrees. Although she knew she had been found out, Jenny let out one more groan. Jenny bowed her head in shame as her mother walked out of the room muttering something in Chinese and shaking her head in irritation.

The plan had failed and Jenny was as irritated with herself as her mother was. "The plan didn't fail," she thought. "I'm the one who failed." And then, Jenny remembered Ms. Candy's story about lambs learning to walk. Jenny pulled out the spy book from under her bed. "Ms. Candy was right," Jenny thought. "I need to keep trying until I figure out a scam that will actually work." Jenny leafed through the book until she found the right chapter. But as quickly as she had opened the book, she closed it again. "Scams can wait," Jenny thought. For now, all she wanted to do was write in her notebook.

Monday, February 8: Sounds Like "Swamp Green"

Jenny dipped her pointer finger into the jar and spread the creamy makeup across her cheek, making sure to blend it into her skin carefully and slowly, just like she had watched her teenage cousin Jing-Wei do whenever they shared a room during family vacations. Last night after her failed high temperature scam, Jenny had selected "MAKE YOURSELF LOOK ILL" from the spy book's list as the next way she would try to fake getting sick. Although Jenny had never put on makeup before, not because she hadn't wanted to, but because her parents thought she was too young, she figured that it would be as easy as the finger painting activities she had always loved in preschool.

The whole process, however, was proving more difficult than Jenny had imagined. Getting the amount of makeup just right was especially tricky. Too much makeup made Jenny look like she had dipped her face into a bowl of flour. Too little makeup made no difference at all. Jenny wondered how her cousin, Jing-Wei, who tended to wear a lot of makeup, managed to look perfect in less time than it took Jenny to get dressed and brush her teeth. Even though Jenny had woken up thirty minutes early to make breakfast, which she then proceeded to wolf down as she was walking back upstairs to her bedroom, it was almost time to leave for school.

"Jenny?" her mother called from the bottom of the stairs, which sent Jenny into a panic. Only half of her face was finished.

"Yes, Mommy?" Jenny answered, as she frantically rubbed makeup onto her chin.

"Time to go," her mother said.

"Okay, Mommy!" Jenny yelled.

"I start the car," her mother said. Seconds later, Jenny heard the garage door open.

No longer concerned with being either careful or slow, Jenny slapped makeup onto the rest of her face in a mad rush that in the end, was exactly as she had predicted, just like her preschool finger painting. When the car horn beeped, Jenny got nervous that her mother would figure out that she was up to something if she didn't come down quickly. Without looking in the mirror for a final examination, Jenny stuffed the makeup jar under her pillow and bolted down the stairs. When her mother beeped the horn a second time, Jenny was already headed out the door with her backpack and lunch box.

The five-mile car ride to school was unusually quiet, even for Jenny and her mother, who normally weren't big talkers. After the weekend's failed attempts at faking sick, Jenny's mother was barely speaking to her. Driving the familiar route through their neighborhood, past the kids waiting for the bus and then onto the main road toward the park next to Haverswell Elementary, her mother continued the silent-treatment as she hummed along with classical music. Jenny, her face glued to the window, watched the outside colors blur together like a rainbow, her thoughts everywhere except the present moment. The music stopped when her mother pulled into the carpool line, but Jenny didn't notice at first because she was too busy watching the morning activity of buses and students and teachers, all trying to make it to where they belonged before the morning bell.

Only when her mother coughed, did Jenny turn her attention toward the front seat. Simultaneously, Jenny realized that the music had been turned off and that her mother was studying her intently in the rearview mirror. She snapped into action. The spy book's instructions were to close your eyes and to pretend to shiver with fever chills if your parents discovered your makeup before you got to school, and Jenny followed these directions to a T. Only when the car door swung open and a smiling teacher cheerfully announced, "Good morning!" did Jenny open her eyes.

As she unbuckled her seat belt, Jenny looked into the rearview mirror again and momentarily locked eyes with her mother. Instead of telling her to have a nice day or saying good bye, Jenny's mother whispered, "Wash it off." The teacher shut the car door and Jenny stood frozen with panic as she watched her mother's car drive away, frightened and shivering for real.

As soon as she heard her mother walk downstairs that morning, Jenny had snuck out of her room and tiptoed across the hall to her parents' bedroom, a place she was normally forbidden to enter without knocking first. The room looked exactly the same way as it had in every one of their four houses in California, from how the furniture was arranged to the artwork that hung on the walls, so Jenny had known exactly where to find her mother's makeup.

The two hundred year-old antique Chinese desk that had belonged to Jenny's great-grandmother was worn in places, but Jenny still thought it was the most beautiful thing her family owned. She figured that a few bumps and bruises weren't all that bad for something that had not only crossed the Pacific Ocean from China on a freight ship, but had also survived five different moves in America. The top of the desk was painted red and contained a three-paneled mirror and a ceramic dish that held her mother's special-occasion perfume bottles.

The front of the desk was divided into two longer side panels with elaborately carved edges. The left side had been hand-painted with a scene depicting the Chinese tale of The Iron Rod. Although she was in a rush, Jenny took a moment to study the painting.

The Iron Rod story is about Li Bai, a lazy young boy who skips school to wander into the forest. He meets an old lady by the river who is tirelessly grinding an iron rod into a sewing needle. Because the iron rod is so big and a needle is so small, he seems confused by her behavior. The old lady tells Li Bai that if she keeps grinding, each day the rod will get thinner and thinner, and eventually become a needle, just like if he studies every day, eventually he will become smarter.

Apparently, the young boy was so inspired by the old lady's wisdom that he not only went on to become a good student, but he turned out to be one of China's best-known poets. Jenny's father recounted The Iron Rod story every time her report card came home, but it wasn't until she heard Ms. Candy's story about the baby lambs learning to walk, that she viewed it as something other than an annoying lesson about how hard work leads to success.

Pulling open the top right-hand drawer, Jenny breathed a sigh of relief when she saw the makeup jar. What Jenny wasn't expecting, however, was to find a picture that she had never seen before, one where she was much younger with chubby pink cheeks and a big smile. Jenny doubted if her mother could ever imagine that cute, innocent little girl would turn into an eleven-year-old who would steal from her.

Once she got back to her own bedroom, Jenny had begun to apply the makeup, but she didn't look pale enough. The spy book had suggested mixing green-tinted makeup together with the regular cream one, but Jenny hadn't found any of this color in her mother's drawer. She was about to give up on the whole plan when the idea to use green oil paint popped into her head. After leafing through her paint box, Jenny found the perfect color, "Swamp Green." The only swamp Jenny had ever seen was actually on the Pirates of the Caribbean ride at Disneyland in California, which she remembered as eerie, and filled with lots of slime-covered props and dead-looking things. Jenny opened the paint cap and grinned. "Swamp Green" was exactly the look she was going for.

In the girl's bathroom mirror at school, however, Jenny realized that the "Swamp Green" mix made her look more silly than sickly, like a cross between two classic Halloween costumes. The streaky green globs covering her face looked like big witches' warts and the blobs of mixture that had dripped onto her neck like Frankenstein's freakish bolts. Until she looked at herself in the bathroom mirror, Jenny had never understood her cousin, Jing-Wei's, claim that the secret to great-looking makeup was "good lighting." She wasn't sure if the light in her bedroom or the car or the school bathroom was to blame for her messed up makeup job. All Jenny knew was that though the first steps of her plan to get out of the piano recital had worked, now, something had gone horribly wrong.

The hallway noise was diminishing, which Jenny knew meant that the morning bell would ring any moment. Recklessly, she began to rub off the makeup, but it stuck to her face like glue. Even when she tried using a wet paper towel, it wouldn't come off. Scraping the heaviest concentrated parts with her nails proved to be somewhat successful, but the downside was that her hands, in addition to most of her face, were now green and sticky. A teacher yelled, "Hurry! School's starting!" to another student in the hallway and Jenny's urgency to avoid a tardy outweighed her concern about her appearance. As she threw away the green-stained paper towels into the trash can, Jenny avoided looking at herself in the mirror as she hurried to class. Sometimes, Jenny thought, it was easier to avoid the truth.

At morning meeting, Ms. Candy reminded the class of the three fun things coming up toward the end of the week. The only person who showed much excitement about Friday's Spelling Bee was Nadia, who went into detail about the new dress her mother had bought her for the occasion. The boasting caused Aidan to groan and roll his eyes. Nadia stared at him angrily for stealing her spotlight. The Valentine's Day Celebration got a mixed response. While everyone was thrilled for the spread of cupcakes, cookies and candy, only a handful of students, including Jenny, seemed to be looking forward to the card exchange. Jenny had a feeling that these students, like her, had already finished making their valentines, and that the others would be scraping their cards together in a panic the night before.

What did trouble Jenny, though, was that she only had a small amount of time to secretly figure out how to get Mr. Short and Ms. Candy to admit their feelings for each other before Valentine's Day. The Fifth-Grade Soccer Game was the one event that the entire class agreed was a true treat. Although she was much more subdued than usual, Lilly managed to join in the cheering, encouraged by Tyler's sympathetic hand on her shoulder.

Ms. Candy also announced to the class that she had both good news and bad news to share with them. Aidan screamed, "Bad news first!"

Even louder, Tyler yelled, "No, good news first!"

Nadia shouted, "Bad news! Bad news!" Jenny laughed to herself as she noted one more thing that Aidan and Nadia agreed on.

Lilly high-fived Tyler and they yelled, "GOOD NEWS!" in unison so deafeningly that Jenny thought Ms. Candy was going to consent, just to put an end to the noise.

But instead, Ms. Candy walked to the chalkboard and said, "We're gonna vote, y'all. Fair's fair." Jenny voted for "bad news first" and she was pleased when it won. Terrible news wouldn't cut quite as deeply if Jenny knew she could stop the bleeding, if only momentarily, with a Band-Aid of good news. Ms. Candy walked back to the rug and sat down on her rocking chair. "The bad news is that we're still dealin' with our writing problem," Ms. Candy said, the class hanging on her every word. "Principal Brimstone and I have decided that the person who is destroying school supplies is plum out of chances."

Nadia stared at Aidan, which caused some of the other kids to do the same. It wasn't the first time since Jenny had arrived at

Haverswell Elementary that Aidan looked like he didn't want the attention, but it was the only time that he seemed scared—truly, completely scared—by it. Jenny wanted them to direct their suspicious stares away from Aidan and toward their seemingly-perfect classmate sitting front and center of the rug, Nadia. At that moment, Jenny realized that she would have to figure out how to stop Nadia and save Aidan more quickly than she had planned.

"Suspension," announced Jack, as he shook his head in disbelief. "Brutal."

"You're right," said Ms. Candy. "Whoever is writing on school property will not only be suspended, but the suspension will be listed on their permanent record." The class looked glum, much more so than after the reminder about the spelling bee. Jenny was happy when Ms. Candy quickly said, "All this bad news has got me as ill as a hornet. I'll give y'all the good news now."

When Ms. Candy picked up the class suggestion box, Jenny's stomach flip-flopped back and forth with alternating feelings of

JEAN RAMSDEN

anxiousness and excitement. She could barely breathe. "Finally," Ms. Candy announced, "a great suggestion! Or maybe I should say 'suggestions' because last Friday, I got twenty-somethin' that said the same exact thing." Tanner was staring at Jenny and she wondered if her blush-red cheeks were giving away her secret. "I don't know who's been up to what, but it doesn't much matter," Ms. Candy continued. "A great suggestion is a great suggestion, and so our class will get to play the 'Sounds Like Game' today."

The only thing that kept Jenny from feeling completely victorious because her fake suggestion box notes had actually worked, was that Tanner had begun looking over at her every few seconds, almost as if he was trying to tell her something. Ms. Candy asked, "Tanner, everything okay?" which caused the whole class to turn in his direction. Since Jenny was sitting next to Tanner, this meant that the class had a good view of her, as well. With nowhere to hide from the stares, both Tanner and Jenny fidgeted in their seats.

Nadia screwed her face up disgustedly at Jenny and snickered, "You know you have green all over you face, right?" Jenny gulped. With the many morning announcements and the anticipation surrounding the suggestion box, Jenny had completely forgotten that her face was splotched with green makeup. The bad news was that now, this fact was obvious to everyone. The good news was that no one could see the real color of her face, which was hot and red with the kind of fire that only complete embarrassment was capable of producing.

"Jenny, honey, come with me into my office," directed Ms. Candy as she led Jenny out of the room. "Class, practice your spelling word lists at your seats. We won't be just a minute."

In the shared fifth-grade office, Ms. Candy moved an apple critter off her chair and sat Jenny down in its place. She began rifling through her giant hot pink purse until she found what she was looking for, makeup remover wipes. Ms. Candy told Jenny to close her eyes and ever so gently, she began to clean her face. After a few minutes, Ms. Candy said, "I remember the first time I tried makeup back when I was about your age. I looked like a circus clown!" When Jenny translated what Ms. Candy had said, she let out a little laugh, but immediately regretted it and squeezed her eyes closed as tightly as she could. But Ms. Candy only laughed and said, "Oh, don't worry. I did look pretty silly!" Wiping Jenny's forehead, she said, "But then I got into beauty pageants, and puttin' on makeup got to be as easy for me as sliding off a greasy log backward."

Ms. Candy pulled another wipe out of the container and said, "The truth is, I'm just a big kid who still likes to play dress up!" Jenny was glad to be able to have her eyes closed so that she could concentrate on what Ms. Candy was saying without worrying about making eye contact. "I'll let you in on a little secret. Most of the time, I'd rather be with kids than adults. They're much more fun!"

Ms Candy sighed, "Of course, someone to watch old movies with would be nice!" and Jenny wondered if she was thinking of Mr. Short.

"All better," announced Ms. Candy. And when Jenny opened her eyes, indeed she was, and not just because all the green makeup was gone. Although she had failed to convince anyone that she was ill, Jenny had succeeded in finding someone she could trust, Ms. Candy. This was more important to her than anything. "What do you say we get back to class and play that game you suggested?" she asked Jenny. Jenny smiled back, as if it didn't matter that she had been found out.

As they walked out of the office together, Ms. Candy stopped and said, "One more thing, Jenny," and suddenly, Jenny knew that the kindness would now be followed by getting in trouble for writing the notes. Her stomach tightened. She dreaded "Good News Then Bad News" situations. Ms. Candy pulled out the lost purple and gold hair bow from her pocket. With a wink and a smile, she said, "I do believe this is yours," as she handed it over.

Jenny and Ms. Candy returned to the class. Any inclination to tease Jenny about her "Swamp Green" face seemed to have been replaced by "Sounds Like Game" excitement. When Ms. Candy asked, "Y'all ready to play?" the class cheered and Jenny breathed a sigh of relief. Ms. Candy said, "Today, we're gonna talk about the word 'like.' Can anyone tell me two ways to use this word?"

Tyler jumped out of his chair and did a touchdown victory dance while he shouted, "I LIKE Carolina football!"

The class shouted, "C-A-R-O-L-I-N-A! Fight. Fight. GoooOOOOOOO Gamecocks!"

Ms. Candy laughed. "Yes! Great example, Tyler. 'Like' can mean that you enjoy something." Tyler nodded. "Who knows another way 'like' can be used?"

Matter-of-factly, Nadia said, "Carolina football stinks like a skunk." The class booed

Nadia's answer, but she just rolled her eyes and said, "That's what my mother says about my father's favorite team."

"Another great example," said Ms. Candy, "that I don't think any of us will forget!" The class started to boo again, but Ms. Candy stopped them and said, "Nadia's right. 'Like' can be used to describe things that are simi- lar." Ms. Candy continued, "There's one way that 'like' is not used correctly."

Lilly raised her hand and sighed, "Guilty."

"That's okay, Lilly. And, you're right. 'Like' is used incorrectly as a verbal pause." Most of the students looked confused.

"A verbal what? I don't get it," said Jack, shaking his head.

"A 'verbal pause' is a fancy pants word for when you fill in the silence between words with 'um' or 'er' or 'you know' or 'like,'" ex- plained Ms. Candy.

"Like, um, now I, er, get it, you know!" yelled Aidan and the class broke into laugh- ter.

"My heavenly days, Aidan! Another great example!" said Ms. Candy and she flashed him a thumbs up. Not used to getting attention for good behavior, it took Aidan a few perplexed moments to realize that what he said had been not only funny but helpful, as well. He beamed with happiness. "Now we're gonna play the 'Sounds Like Game' so not just Lilly, but everyone, can stop using 'like' incorrectly."

For the rest of the day, whenever a student heard someone else using "like" as a verbal pause they got to yell out, "SOUNDS LIKE!" The person who slipped-up had to stop whatever they were doing and go to the front of the room and look up one of the spelling words in Ms. Candy's thesaurus. After they found a word that meant the same thing as the spelling word, the person had to write it on the chalkboard.

The class loved the "Sounds Like Game" primarily because they got to bust their friends. Although Nadia never got busted herself, she loved catching others' mistakes. Jenny had never seen her so happy. Ms. Candy loved the game because in addition to listening to each other, the students started paying attention to their own speech so that by the end of the day, "like" was being used much less incorrectly.

Lilly was busted the most out of everybody, so much so that eventually, Ms. Candy gave Lilly her own thesaurus and dry erase board. Jenny thought Lilly was a good sport about having to do so much work. Each time that Lilly had to stop and look up a word, Jenny smiled. She knew from her own experience learning English, that you could be told something a hundred times, but unless you truly understood the problem, you wouldn't change.

Lilly was off to a good start. Jenny wondered exactly how long it took a baby lamb to learn to walk or for the woman in The Iron Rod to make the sewing needle. She only hoped that Lilly's "like" problem would be gone quickly, in time for Saturday's soccer game.

At home, Jenny climbed the stairs to her room and thought about the day. The bad news was that the makeup hadn't convinced anyone that she was ill, which meant she was still going to have to perform the difficult piece in the piano recital. The good news was that she had succeeded at getting Ms. Candy to play the "Sounds Like Game" in class, and that already, Lilly's "like" problem seemed to be improving.

When she opened the door to her room, Jenny got another bit of good news. A hundred-piece makeup set with eye shadow, lipstick, blush, and powder in every color imaginable had been placed in the middle of her bed. Jenny's mother hadn't said much to her on the ride home and Jenny had assumed that she was still mad about the face-slapping, the fake temperature and this morning's green makeup disaster. Jenny's heart filled with kindness for the second time that day; Ms. Candy wasn't the only one who cared about her.

Jenny looked at her notebook and then back at the new makeup set. Writing could wait for a few minutes, Jenny decided. She wanted to try on her new makeup, especially the puce-colored lipstick.

TUESDAY, FEBRUARY 9:
HOW TO WRITE
A SECRET NOTE

This Tuesday, when Ms. Candy marched into the classroom twirling a baton and wearing her knee-high black boots and majorette outfit, Jenny knew exactly what to expect, even without looking at the numbers on her teacher's two-foot-tall hat. She wasn't excited about having to endure another embarrassing math race, but Jenny couldn't help but smile at Ms. Candy's peppiness. "Good morning, class! Time for Tuesday Times Tables! TIME for Tuesday TIMES Tables!" sang Ms. Candy, her face glowing with cheeriness as she blew her whistle. "FWEEEEEEEEEEE!" Like a real illness, and not one of Jenny's fake ones, Ms. Candy's energy was contagious. The baton rolled back and forth along her elbow and she said, "Let's get into our Tuesday Times Tables rows! Remember, the easiest math problem will go to the person in the back seat and the hardest one will go to the person in the front seat."

Just like last week, everyone hurried to change seats except Nadia and Aidan. Although no one asked her to move, Jenny stood up and started to walk toward the front seat in her row just as Ms. Candy marched past. As she twirled the baton above her head, Ms. Candy leaned in Jenny's direction and said quietly, "Jenny, why don't you try the back seat this week?" Jenny breathed a sigh of relief. The idea of a math race still made her anxious, but at least she would get the easiest problem and the most time to solve it. Like a cannonball, Ms. Candy's baton shot up over her hat. As it came sailing down, Ms. Candy twisted her left hand behind her back and winked at Jenny as she caught it.

Marching to the head of the class, Ms. Candy blew her whistle again and said, "Ten seconds to make your final order changes before the race starts!" Jenny rushed into the seat at the back of her row. Aidan, who was now sitting next to her, pounded his desk and announced, "Welcome to the best seats in the class!" Even though she didn't totally understand Aidan's joke, Jenny smiled back politely, as she nervously squeezed her eraser like she was molding a chunk of pink clay. Aidan leaned toward her and with a sly grin said, "Listen, we get the easiest problem and no one pays attention to you back here."

But at this moment, Jenny felt like she was actually getting lots of attention. The more Aidan talked to her, the more Jenny felt like a giant spotlight was shining down on her, which made her squeeze the eraser harder and harder. "You'll be fine, trust me," Aidan assured her as he gently patted her shoulder. This made Jenny squeeze her eraser so hard that it jumped right out of her fingers and onto his desk. As he handed the eraser back to her, Aidan chuckled and said, "The problem is so easy, you definitely won't need one of these."

The math race worked the same way as last week. Aidan, Jenny and the other students in the back flipped over the worksheets when Ms. Candy blew her whistle and yelled, "Go!"

$$11 \times 5 = ?$$

With one quick look at the problem, Jenny realized that Aidan was exactly right. In a few seconds, she wrote down the answer and passed the worksheet forward. In the end, Nadia's row won again, but Jenny didn't really care. Aidan's comforting words had helped her not to panic. And, Jenny hadn't let down her row because Ms. Candy had allowed her to sit in the seat she truly belonged in. These two acts of kindness were more important to Jenny than any brief moment of classroom glory.

After the Tuesday Times Tables race, everyone went back to their seats. Lilly leaned toward Jenny and admitted, "I'm glad that's over with!" Turning toward Lilly, who still had the thesaurus and dry erase board covered with spelling words on her desk, Jenny smiled, barely able to contain her excitement. She had proof that the "Sounds Like Game" was working.

Jenny wasn't the only one who noticed that Lilly had spoken clearly, without saying "like." Balancing the baton on the top of her hat, Ms. Candy applauded. Nadia sat with her mouth hung open, annoyed that she didn't get to bust Lilly. With a mix of surprise and pride spreading across her face, Lilly jumped out of her chair and ran over to Tyler. High-fiving, they both cheered, "YES!"

At lunch, Aidan's plastic lunch tray crashed down on the table with a little less force than it had done in the week prior. Only a few of Jenny's peas jumped out of their container and just one of Mr. Short's apple slices ended up in his soup. Taking a seat two places over from Jenny, Aidan asked, "Can I sit here?" And, because she wanted to return the kindness Aidan had shown her before the math race, Jenny gathered up all her courage and spoke only her second word since arriving at Haverswell Elementary. "Yes," she agreed.

"See, what did I tell you about the math problem? Easy, right?" asked Aidan. Jenny nodded. "You even finished before me!" With a mouth full of sandwich, he laughed, "Which isn't saying much since math isn't exactly my best subject."

Although Jenny wanted to tell Aidan that her best subjects were art and comic books, and not anything to do with school, she only managed, "Yes."

"You, too?" Aidan asked. Jenny nodded. "I figured as much since Ms. Candy moved you into the back row." Aidan took a drink of his juice and said, "Best seats in the class, right?" This time, Aidan's joke made sense to Jenny and she laughed right along with him.

Jenny and Aidan finished their lunches in silence while the rest of the cafeteria buzzed with noise. Only when Mr. Short left to get his daily cupcakes from the vending machine, did Aidan start to speak again. Sorrowfully, as if he was talking about some incurable disease, he said, "See, I'm an only child. So, you can't blame me if I don't have anyone to study with." When Jenny nodded, Aidan said, "You, too?"

Even though she had never talked about being an only child with anyone, Jenny said, "Yes." Sharing this much detail about her life with Aidan made her frightened but also, relieved. Someone was finally interested.

"How about your parents? Divorced?" Aidan asked coldly. Jenny only shook her head slightly and shifted her eyes toward the table. Revealing that she was an only child was one thing, but talking about her parents was something entirely different and in her family, considered disrespectful. "Oh," Aidan said quietly. "I didn't mean to embarrass you."

Despite how harsh Aidan could appear at times, moments like this and like the math race, proved to Jenny that he did have a gentle side, too. She felt terrible about how Aidan was being unfairly blamed for destroying the school supplies because as the class prankster, he was everyone's obvious choice. Jenny thought it was similar to how everyone in her class except Ms. Candy and Aidan assumed that she was smart or the piano teacher assumed she was a musical genius, just because she was Chinese.

What Jenny wanted most, was for people to know the truth about who she really was. As she studied the sadness in Aidan's eyes, she wondered if he wanted the same thing. Moving to the seat next to Aidan, Jenny did her best imitation of Ms. Candy's comforting smile. Jenny wanted Aidan to know that he could count on her as a friend, which to her, meant that her only job was to listen.

Aidan took a deep breath and then said, "Yeah, my parents got divorced a few years ago, which kind of messed things up. At least I didn't have to hear them fight all the time, though. Know what I mean?"

Jenny had never heard her parents argue, but she lied and said, "Yes."

"At first it was great. Man, did I get a lot of presents!" Aidan remembered excitedly. "And dessert at every meal!" Suddenly, Aidan looked away and Jenny watched as all the enthusiasm poured out of him. "Then, my mom got a job a few hours away. I really only get to see her over the summer and on holidays."

Even though Jenny wasn't best friends with her mother, she couldn't imagine a day without her. Thinking about this possibility, Jenny's smile lessened. Aidan said reassuringly, "I miss my mom and everything, but it was cool for it to be just me and my dad. We watched sports together, made dinner together and we got really into video games. It was pretty awesome." Taking his last sip of juice Aidan sighed, "Then he met my stepmom." Squeezing his juice box until it fit in his hand, he said angrily, "She ruined everything."

Then, Aidan smashed his juice box, which sent the straw flying right into Mr. Short's glasses at the other end of the table. With a mouth full of cupcake, Mr. Short looked at Aidan suspiciously. "Now the only reason anybody pays attention to me is when I get in trouble," Aidan snickered uncomfortably. "I get a few laughs, and my dad and my step-mom spend all their time talking about what a bad kid I am." As Aidan shrugged his shoulders he said coolly, "Bad attention is still attention, right?"

Jenny reached her arm toward Aidan to pat him on the back like he had done to her before the math race. But just then, the dismissal bell rang. Everyone flooded out of the cafeteria, including Aidan, who bolted ahead, leaving Jenny alone and his smashed juice box on the table for someone else to clean up.

Aidan was already in his seat in the back row when Jenny got back to the classroom. As she walked past him, he placed a folded note in her hand. Jenny hurried to her seat and shoved the note into her desk.

Aidan's lunch visits and his kindness during the math race were starting to make sense. Jenny started to think that maybe he was the Secret Note Writer. On the other hand, Aidan's restless personality didn't seem to match the calming words that each note always contained. Somehow, Jenny couldn't picture Aidan telling her, "It's all good," without also adding something funny. Plus, Jenny wasn't exactly sure how Aidan had delivered them from the back of the room to her desk in the middle without anyone noticing, especially Ms. Candy.

When Ms. Candy started writing their lesson on the chalkboard, her back turned to the class, Jenny quickly pulled out the note. This time, the outside of the note only contained a messily written instruction: "OPEN IT UP!" Jenny unfolded the note under her desk and gasped when she read it. Moments later, Aidan began coughing so loudly that Ms. Candy stopped writing to ask, "Everything okay, Aidan?"

Aidan grabbed his throat and said, "Throat tickle," in a dramatically scratchy voice that made Nadia roll her eyes and Ms. Candy study him with caution, as if she knew he might be up to something.

"I'm almost done, y'all," Ms. Candy said and she continued writing. "Keep your pants on!"

Aidan let out an even louder cough, a noise that sounded more like a gag, and Jenny knew that she should probably do what the note said or else he would cause an even bigger commotion. As quietly as possible, Jenny folded the note back up and then tossed it onto Lilly's desk. For the next few minutes, the note was passed around the class to every person but Nadia. Each person had the same reaction, disbelief.

By the time the note landed on Jack's desk, Ms. Candy had finished writing. "Now we're gonna do a writing activity using words from the spelling bee list," she announced to the class. But no one was paying attention. They were all waiting to see who would walk over to the trash can first.

Ms. Candy was explaining the writing activity when Jack, following the note's instructions, made his way to the trash can. When he bent down and began picking up coins from the ground, everyone realized that whoever wrote the note was right—someone had accidentally thrown away money. After he gathered all the coins, Jack started digging through the trash. Soon, paper towel scraps, used tissues, food wrappers, dirty plastic bags and pencil shavings were flying everywhere.

"Jack," asked Ms. Candy, "what on earth are you searchin' through the trash for?" Jack simply held up a handful of coins as his excuse. Ms. Candy walked over to the almost empty trash can and peered in. "Did someone accidentally throw away their lunch money?" she asked the class.

Jack looked in the trash can and shouted, "Dude! There's a bunch of money on the bottom!" The class was on the edge of their seats. "At least five dollars worth!"

"Epic!" yelled Tyler.

"Jack, honey, can you collect all those coins?" Ms. Candy asked. "We'll count 'em up and get 'em back to their rightful owner."

The class watched excitedly as Jack threw himself into the task. But after a few minutes of searching, he didn't manage to produce a single penny.

"What are you doing in there, digging for China?" Tyler joked which made everyone laugh, especially Jenny, who immediately understood. China was a long way from Haverswell, South Carolina, which Jenny knew firsthand because she had been to both places.

"They're stuck," Jack said. He shook the can up and down and then tried scraping out the coins. "Man, they won't budge!"

"Give'r here," said Ms. Candy and Jack passed her the trash can. Ms. Candy gave it a shake, but strangely, it didn't rattle with coins. When she turned it upside down, nothing fell out, even after she hit the bottom with her baton. In one last attempt, she reached deep into the trash can and tried to pull out the coins with her long pink fingernails. "Oooooh!" Ms. Candy screamed. She had tried to stay quiet, but when the end of her nail ripped off it had hurt too much not to cry out in pain. "My finger!"

Mr. Short came running in and surveyed the scene. Dressed in her majorette outfit, Ms. Candy was sucking her injured finger,

Jack was holding a handful of coins from the floor and Aidan had begun to laugh hysterically. Mr. Short used the classroom phone to call Principal Brimstone and when he waddled in, Ms. Candy pulled her finger out of her mouth. "Aidan superglued coins to the bottom of the trash can," Ms. Candy said exhaustedly.

"I see," Principal Brimstone sighed. And then he turned to Aidan and said, "To make up for your bad choices, you'll have to empty all the trash cans in the school before you are allowed to return to class."

"The engine's runnin', Aidan, but sometimes it's like nobody's driving," said Ms. Candy. Pointing to the trash can with her injured finger she said, "You're a better person than that."

And, perhaps because Aidan had revealed his nice side or maybe because she felt sad about his parents' divorce, Jenny felt the urge to stick up for him, too. Jenny wanted Aidan to know that Ms. Candy wasn't the only person who felt like there was more to him than silly class pranks. Suddenly, Jenny stood up and amid the silence, she shouted, "Yes!"

Principal Brimstone, Ms. Candy, Mr. Short and the rest of the class turned to face Jenny, who instantaneously became the only student who had ever stood up for Aidan. In that moment, Jenny was barely aware that anyone except her and Aidan existed, the attention failing to embarrass her like usual. Aidan didn't run off like at lunch. Instead, he smiled back at her and said, "Thanks."

After Aidan left with Principal Brimstone, Jenny had trouble concentrating. While the class was busy with their writing assignment, Jenny was daydreaming about what might have happened if Jack had shaken the trash can and Aidan hadn't glued down the coins. She imagined the pennies, nickels, dimes and quarters flying into the air like confetti and then scattering everywhere once they landed, bouncing off desks and walls or spinning on the ground like tops. What was spinning now, however, were not coins but her mind, which was filled with bits and pieces of her conversations with Aidan, especially the part about ways to get attention.

As she wrote down a jumbled sentence for her writing assignment, Jenny realized that her spy book scams to get out of the piano recital were really, just the same thing as Aidan's classroom pranks—bad attention. The recital was only five days away and Jenny began to feel more anxious every time she thought about how much of the piano piece she still didn't know. What she needed, Jenny concluded, was a scam that was more extreme than a red face, a high fever or green makeup. Remembering the spy book's list, Jenny thought again about the unglued coins and settled on the perfect one.

For the second time that day, Jenny stood up amongst a silent classroom. Without saying a word, she bumped into her chair and then fell into Lilly's desk.

"Are you okay?" Lilly asked. Jenny had wanted to smile again—Lilly had not used the word "like"—but instead, she just tried to act as dizzy and as confused as possible. Jenny imagined herself as a spinning coin and started twirling around and around until she got so dizzy that she tripped over Nadia's foot and fell to the ground.

"Oh, goodness!" shouted Ms. Candy as she ran to help Jenny. As Ms. Candy pulled her up, Jenny noticed several black markers in Nadia's desk and was relieved that Aidan would be emptying trash cans for the rest of the day. She figured Nadia wouldn't write on any school supplies if there wasn't anyone to blame. Ms. Candy felt Jenny's head. "Well, you're as cool as a glass of iced tea, but somethin's not right," Ms. Candy said. "Come with me, Jenny. Let's get your mama on the phone."

In the shared fifth-grade office, Ms. Candy called Jenny's mother to explain that Jenny had almost fainted, while Jenny looked around her desk and made a game of spotting all her hidden desserts. A butterscotch sticky bun was wedged into Ms. Candy's purse, a half-eaten double chocolate chip muffin sat alongside books, and stuffed under her chair was an almost empty cup that had "Peppermint White Mocha + Extra Whipped Cream" written on the side. The next thing Jenny knew, Mr. Short walked into the office. Ms. Candy had just hung up the phone when she saw him. She ran to her purse, pushed down the butterscotch sticky bun and quickly zipped it shut—right onto her injured finger—before he noticed.

"How's the finger?" Mr. Short said as he gathered a few papers.

Ms. Candy, who never seemed to get embarrassed despite all the crazy things that happened in school, looked at Mr. Short and mumbled, "Just dandy!" with a face as red as Jenny's often turned.

After Mr. Short walked out of the office, Ms. Candy let out a deep breath and yelled, "Oooooh! My poor little finger!" Then she unzipped her purse, pulled out the butterscotch sticky bun and took a giant bite. "Mr. Short would be absolutely disgusted if he knew I ate these things. He's so healthy, eating fruits and vegetables all the time."

Ms. Candy stared dreamily into the distance. "We could never go to dinner together." As she took another bite of the bun, Ms. Candy sighed, "I'm the type of person who just can't resist sweets."

When Jenny's mother picked her up at school, she assumed that their next stop would be home, where she would be able to spend the rest of the week in bed. But Jenny's mother had driven directly to the optometrist's office, where after having her eyes dilated and enduring a thorough eye exam, the doctor had confirmed that Jenny's vision was 20/20—perfect. Although the eye dilation was making everything blurry, for real this time, Jenny concluded that her mother had not exactly believed her clumsy act. She started behaving normally again.

After dinner, Jenny went to her room to research a school project, but she quickly felt her mind wander. She was thinking about Aidan's note and the Secret Note Writer, and then about how she was going to get Ms. Candy and Mr. Short together before Valentine's Day, when an idea popped into her head. Ten minutes later, she pressed "print" on the computer's keyboard. The poem she had just written read,

Roses are red.
Violets are blue.
I LOVE SWEETS.
You do, too.

In her neatest handwriting, she wrote, "TO: MS. CANDY. FROM: MR. SHORT," on the front of the envelope and licked it sealed. As a shy person herself, Jenny knew that sometimes, expressing yourself was hard. Since she had arrived at Haverswell Elementary, Ms. Candy had helped Jenny open up and now Jenny wanted to return the favor, even if it involved a little scheming.

Jenny put the envelope into her backpack. Then she sat down on the bench of her electronic piano and reviewed how the other problems she was trying to solve were progressing. Nadia hadn't destroyed any school supplies this week and Lilly wasn't saying "like" as much. Jenny knew that she should have been happy about the improvements, but she found it hard to celebrate because she still hadn't learned the piano piece.

Jenny thought about the Iron Rod story and Ms. Candy's baby lambs, and then another idea popped into her head. If she wanted to learn how to play her assigned song, she would just have to practice and practice and practice. She plugged her headphones into the piano, stretched out her fingers and turned to the opening movement.

WEDNESDAY, FEBRUARY 10:
TONGUE TIED

Trudging down the stairs one at a time holding onto the railing for support, Jenny felt like she was still asleep. She remembered her alarm ringing earlier, but she couldn't recall getting dressed. Halfway down the stairs, Jenny studied her dirty shirt and the grass-stained knees of her pants and suddenly, everything made sense. She had stayed awake so late practicing for the piano recital that she had fallen asleep in her clothes. Jenny slumped down and rested her head on her knees. Hair from yesterday's braids stuck out

JEAN RAMSDEN

every which way, messy like scarecrow straw.
Jenny closed her eyes and sighed. Changing
into clean clothes and re-braiding her hair
seemed like impossible tasks.

"Jenny?" her mother called from the bottom of the stairs. "You okay?"

Jolted awake, Jenny sat up and said slug-
gishly, "Yes, Mommy. I'll be down in a minute."

Five minutes later, Jenny walked into the
kitchen dressed in a completely new outfit.
With no energy to re-braid her hair, she had
pulled it back into a loose ponytail, which
looked only slightly neater than when she had
first woken up. Although they hardly ever ate
breakfast together, this morning Jenny's
mother sat down and poured them both a
cup of tea as Jenny picked at her fruit plate.

The tea was so soothing that she forgot all
about sipping slowly or purposefully as she
had been taught, and drank the entire cup
without putting it down. Jenny felt her
mother's narrowed eyes studying her. Assum-
ing that her mother was going to bring up
her lack of manners or yesterday's fake faint-

ing or maybe all of her failed scams from the past week, Jenny shifted her eyes toward the table. But, her mother just took a deep breath and repeated, "You okay?"

Jenny's mother wouldn't have been able to hear her practicing past midnight since her headphones were plugged in to her electronic piano, but she would have been proud of her efforts. But because Jenny was afraid of admitting the real reason why she had practiced so long, that she was desperately trying to learn the much too difficult piano piece, Jenny lied and said, "Diarrhea." Then, Jenny sprang from her chair and bolted to the bathroom, clutching her stomach for extra effect.

Alone in the bathroom, Jenny locked the door. Sitting on top of the closed toilet seat, still fully clothed, she sang the South Carolina song over and over again in her head until her mother announced that it was time to go to school. "Okay, Mommy," Jenny yelled. "One minute." After flushing the toilet twice, Jenny pretended to wash her hands while she listened to her mother find her keys.

"I start the car," her mother said.

Jenny came out of the bathroom when she heard the garage door open. Quickly grabbing her backpack, she followed her mother outside. For the second day in row, Jenny got into the car and ended up at the doctor's office.

This time, however, Jenny's mother drove to the city, where everything—the buildings, the amount of people on the streets, the noise—was much bigger than Haverswell, South Carolina, but also much smaller than any of the cities in California where she had lived before. "Something's wrong" were the only words Jenny's mother said to her on the car ride, which made perfect sense when they arrived forty-five minutes later at the Traditional Chinese Medicine doctor.

Jenny only visited a regular family doctor to get shots for school. She had also been to the emergency room in second grade when she was very ill and her fever had reached 105 degrees. Otherwise, Jenny had appointments with the Traditional Chinese Medicine doctor a few times a year, just to make sure everything in her body was working together smoothly. Most kids in the Chinese American Schools that she had attended in California did the same thing as Jenny, but she doubted anyone in Haverswell had ever even heard of Traditional Chinese Medicine except maybe Eddie Wang or a few of the other Chinese mothers at church, who were probably the reason that Jenny's mother had driven all the way to the city to figure out what was wrong with her. The idea that she had been the subject of conversation filled Jenny with utter humiliation.

Doctor Ma greeted Jenny and her mother in Chinese, which meant they would continue to speak the language for the entire visit. Jenny sat on a wooden examination table and when Doctor Ma asked why Jenny's mother had brought her into the office, Jenny's mother repeated what she had said in the car, "Something's wrong."

"We'll figure out if there is an imbalance," Doctor Ma said reassuringly in Chinese.

"Thank you," said Jenny's mother. "Ever since we moved to South Carolina, Jenny has been acting so strangely. I'm very worried." Jenny had not heard her mother as concerned since her emergency room incident in second grade. Immediately, Jenny felt terrible about all the sickness scams. Her mother was actually troubled, and Jenny wanted to cry.

"Let's start with your pulse, Jenny," Doctor Ma instructed. Jenny held out both arms. With his eyes closed, Doctor Ma placed his fingers on Jenny's left wrist and felt her pulse for a few minutes. Then, he studied her right wrist. Doctor Ma did this two more times on each side as Jenny sat quietly, wondering if he had already recognized her imbalance. "And now your tongue, please," Doctor Ma requested. For the next several minutes, Jenny stuck out her tongue as he examined every inch.

"Now," said Doctor Ma to Jenny, "I think it would be helpful to ask you some questions." Jenny gulped. Her throat was dry and her tongue felt heavy from Doctor Ma's pushing and pulling it in every direction. Plus,

Jenny knew that lying to a Traditional Chinese Medicine doctor, someone who was trained to discover the truth, was pointless. She would have to be honest in front of Doctor Ma and her mother.

"Do you have chills?" asked Doctor Ma.

"Yes!" exclaimed Jenny's mother.

Doctor Ma looked at Jenny's mother and said, "Mrs. Liu, please let Jenny answer." He turned to Jenny and repeated the question. "Do you have chills, Jenny?"

Jenny had faked chills on the day she applied the green makeup, but she answered truthfully, "No." Jenny's mother studied her curiously.

"Do you have fevers?" asked Doctor Ma.

"Yes!" exclaimed Jenny's mother.

"Mrs. Liu," said Doctor Ma sternly. "Let Jenny answer the question."

Mrs. Liu turned her eyes away from Doctor Ma's and said, "I'm sorry, Doctor Ma."

"Jenny," asked Doctor Ma. "Do you ever have fevers?"

Since arriving in Haverswell, Jenny had never experienced a real fever. She had only tried to fake one by heating the thermometer. "No," she said.

"I see," said Doctor Ma. "And, do you often sweat?"

Mrs. Liu yelled out, "Oh, never!" and Doctor Ma shook his head in frustration.

Jenny thought about all the times in the last week and a half that she had sweated uncontrollably. On the first day while she waited for Principal Brimstone Jenny remembered sweating so much that she ruined her new shirt. When she had snuck into the classroom to stuff the suggestion box with fake notes, Jenny recalled soaking with sweat as she ran out. In her nightmare about being on stage at the piano recital, Jenny thought about how she sweaty she was when she finally woke up. And, almost every time she got attention in school, Jenny knew that she sweated automatically. "Yes," Jenny answered loudly.

"I see," said Doctor Ma. "And, how is your appetite?"

Jenny remembered how eating so many crullers had upset her stomach. She said, "Not good."

"And, are you going the bathroom and sleeping okay?" said Doctor Ma.

Even though Doctor Ma was no longer listening to her, Jenny's mother said, "Jenny has diarrhea and she's always in her room sleeping."

Ignoring Jenny's mother, Doctor Ma repeated, "So, are you going the bathroom and sleeping okay?"

"I don't have diarrhea," admitted Jenny, avoiding her mother's stares. "I'm in my room a lot, but I'm not sleeping." Jenny thought of her homework and piano practice and art projects and learning the South Carolina song and reading and all the problems she was trying to solve at school and her comic books and especially, all the new people and things she had been forced to learn about because of the move. "I'm busy," Jenny said. "And, I'm very tired."

For several minutes, Doctor Ma studied Jenny intently. Confessing everything had been both exhausting and energizing, and Jenny tried her hardest not to cry in front of Doctor Ma or her mother, who was looking even more distressed by the minute. "Please excuse me," Doctor Ma told them. On the other side of the room, hundreds of clear jars containing herbs of every color lined the shelves. Jenny heard Doctor Ma begin to create her tea mixture. When Doctor Ma returned, he handed Jenny's mother the concoction and instructed Jenny to drink it two times a day for the next several weeks. "This will help," he said kindly.

"Thank you, Doctor Ma," said Jenny's mother. He nodded with approval.

"Thank you," said Jenny.

Doctor Ma smiled. He took Jenny's hand into his own and she noticed that it was neither too hot nor too cold, it wasn't sticky or dry, and that his skin felt as soft as a blanket. "You must be quiet," he said. Jenny, who thought of herself as the quietest person she knew, looked confused. His comment was almost laughable. Bringing Jenny's hand up to her lips, Doctor Ma said, "Not quiet here."

Then raising her hand to her forehead he said, "Quiet here." Doctor Ma chuckled. "Too noisy!" Jenny smiled shyly. "Do you understand, Jenny?" he asked.

Jenny did understand what Doctor Ma meant. She also knew that she was done with faking sick. As she thought of the Secret Note Writer, she said tentatively, "It's all good."

"Jenny!" snapped her mother. "I'm sorry for her rudeness, Doctor Ma."

"Jenny is exactly right, Mrs. Liu," Doctor Ma said, smiling. "She shouldn't worry so much. It's all good!" Doctor Ma laughed from deep within his belly.

When Jenny arrived at school after the doctor's appointment, her class was outside at recess practicing for the upcoming Fifth-Grade Soccer Game. She put her backpack in her cubby and looked around the classroom to figure out what activities she had missed. On the chalkboard, Ms. Candy had written, "PRACTICE SPELLING BEE." Jenny felt relieved that she hadn't had to participate, especially today, when she was tired and emotional. Underneath, Ms. Candy had written, "1ST PLACE: NADIA. 2ND PLACE: LILLY."

When Jenny realized that she had read correctly, she leapt high into the air in celebration. Lilly was no longer "The World's Worst Speller" as she had claimed on Jenny's first day at school. The "Sounds Like Game" had forced Lilly to look up the spelling words so many times, that now, in addition to not saying "like" very much, she was almost as good as Nadia at spelling. Lilly was one of the best spellers in the class.

As she unpacked her backpack, Jenny came across the envelope containing the poem she had written to Ms. Candy pretending to be Mr. Short. Figuring that it was the perfect time to plant it for Ms. Candy because she was alone in the classroom, Jenny walked up to her teacher's desk. It was covered with papers and books, so Jenny decided to place the envelope on Ms. Candy's chair so it wouldn't get lost in the clutter.

Just as she was pulling out the chair, Jenny heard a noise and froze. At first, she thought it might be a mouse, but then Jenny was able to make out footsteps, which were too quiet to belong to Mr. Short and didn't sound like they were coming from the shared office. Quietly, Jenny began to tiptoe out of the room with the envelope still in her hand. Whoever it was, Jenny didn't want to get caught.

As she walked past the classroom bathroom, Jenny heard someone inside crying. Suddenly, the door swung open and the next thing Jenny knew, she was standing face to face with Nadia. For a brief moment, both girls stood tongue tied, regarding each other's intentions. Jenny stared at the black markers that Nadia held and Nadia stared at the envelope that Jenny held. It was Nadia who broke the silence first.

"Allergies," she said, pointing to her tear-stained red eyes. She did not provide an excuse for the black markers and Jenny did not mention them.

Holding up the envelope, Jenny said, "Special delivery." Nadia did not question that the front of the envelope said, "TO: MS. CANDY. FROM: MR. SHORT."

"Well, I'm going to go back into the bathroom to blow my nose," Nadia said. When Jenny didn't move, Nadia said with intent, "So, you can go deliver the letter now." Nadia coughed and said, "I'm closing the door now," her words almost shooing Jenny away. When the bathroom door closed, Jenny was certain that neither she nor Nadia would ever mention the fact that they both knew exactly what the other one was up to. With Nadia in the bathroom again, Jenny ran to Ms. Candy's desk and placed the envelope on her chair. And then, she ran all the way to the field, where she joined her class for soccer practice.

When the class returned from outside, Nadia was already sitting at her desk. She was blowing her nose, but Jenny didn't know if she was doing this for dramatic effect to explain the allergies or because she had been crying again. As Jack passed Nadia's desk, he said, "Ewww. What's on your hand, Nadia?" Nadia looked down at her hands, which were smudged with black marker.

Nadia whined, "There's writing everywhere in this classroom! I can't help it if I lean against a desk and black gets all over my dress or I pick up an eraser and suddenly, my hands are covered!" Nadia began to cry much differently than she had in the bathroom. Jenny could tell that this time, the cries were actually fake. "Ms. Candy?" asked Nadia. "May I please be excused to get cleaned up?"

"Of course, sugar," said Ms. Candy as she tried to settle the class for their next activity. Nadia walked toward the classroom bathroom and glared at Jack as she passed his desk. The second she opened the door, Nadia screamed, which sent Ms. Candy running.

"Well, dog my cats, there's spelling words written all over the bathroom!" Ms. Candy exclaimed, her jaw dropped to the floor. Nadia stood in the middle of the bathroom, crying and surrounded by spelling words written in black marker. Ms. Candy and a crowd of students evaluated the situation in disbelief.

When Aidan yelled, "Oh, man," a few people looked at him suspiciously. After that, Aidan tried his best not to look guilty by staying quiet. Repositioning herself next to him, Jenny smiled supportively. Ms. Candy's attention shifted back and forth between Aidan and the part of the chalkboard that read, "1ST PLACE: NADIA," and then, to Nadia. Jenny wondered if Ms. Candy was thinking the same thing that she already knew—Aidan could have never written the words so neatly or spelled them all correctly, but that the person who had won the spelling bee every year and who always seemed to be getting covered in black marker, Nadia, very well could have.

Both Principal Brimstone and the school janitor were immediately called into the classroom. While the janitor scrubbed the spelling words off the bathroom walls, Ms. Candy huddled with Principal Brimstone in the office discussing what to do next. When they were done, Ms. Candy said, "Principal Brimstone and I have a real good idea about who's doing all the writin'. In fact, we've got it narrowed down to two people in this class." Everyone began to look around at each other, trying to figure out if they were sitting next to the potential suspects.

"Have y'all ever heard the phrase 'A wolf in sheep's clothing'?" Ms. Candy asked the class. Most of the students raised their hands or nodded. Looking between Aidan and Nadia, Ms. Candy said, "So y'all know that sometimes, appearances can be deceiving." Jenny didn't understand what Ms. Candy meant, but her tone made it seem that her teacher was close to discovering the truth about the writing situation.

When Principal Brimstone said goodbye to the class, Ms. Candy walked toward her desk and sighed, "After this mess, I've got to sit myself down a spell. Y'all do some silent reading." As soon as Ms. Candy passed the front row, Nadia spun her head around and shot a wicked look at Jenny. Jenny hadn't tattled to Ms. Candy about catching Nadia in the bathroom with the black markers, and so she took Doctor Ma's advice and tried to not worry so much about what Nadia thought.

"Quiet," Jenny said to herself, just as Ms. Candy let out a little gasp. When Jenny looked up, Ms. Candy was opening the envelope that she had placed on her chair. While everyone else in the class was absorbed in their books, Jenny watched Ms. Candy slowly begin to blush as she read the typed poem.

As if on cue, Mr. Short walked into the classroom, and said glumly, "I heard about the writing in the bathroom."

Ms. Candy quickly hid the note behind her back and giggled, "It's very SWEET of you to check on me, Mr. Short!"

"Of...of course, Ms. Candy," said Mr. Short, looking confused as he adjusted his glasses. Sounding tongue tied, he mumbled, "Well, I...I just wanted to make sure you were okay."

"Very SWEET. Very SWEET, indeed," Ms. Candy gushed.

As Mr. Short walked out of the room confusedly shaking his head, Ms. Candy read the poem again and smiled. Jenny smiled right along with Ms. Candy because her plan to help the teachers discover the truth about each other's love of sweets, and for each other, was working. Now that Ms. Candy knew how Mr. Short felt, Jenny wondered how she could get Mr. Short to know how Ms. Candy felt. Although Jenny wasn't supposed to be worrying, her mind raced for the rest of the day with ideas about how to solve the problem.

At home, Jenny's mother delivered her the prescribed tea as she was practicing the piano piece. Jenny felt good about learning the opening movement, but the middle of the piece was proving even more difficult than Jenny had originally thought. She was trying not to get frustrated with herself.

"Drink tea," Jenny's mother instructed. Before closing the door, she said gently, "Don't worry about piano." And tonight, with Doctor Ma and her mother's calming words helping her to relax, Jenny didn't. As she slowly and purposefully sipped her tea, just as she was taught, Jenny wrote in her notebook instead.

Thursday, February 11:
Coming Clean

"Good morning, good morning, good morning!" beamed Ms. Candy as she danced into the classroom, as light as a feather. "We've got an exciting few days ahead, don't we?" she said, immediately setting off waves of animated conversation. "Who's ready for tomorrow's spelling bee?"

When Ms. Candy had asked this question on Jenny's first day, Nadia was the only person who had seemed excited. But today, the entire class cheered. The chalkboard still read, "1ST PLACE: NADIA. 2ND PLACE:

LILLY." Looking over at the practice spelling bee results, Ms. Candy eagerly rubbed her hands together and said, "I think we've got a real contest this year!"

"Go Lilly!" rooted Tyler.

"I'm like—" Lilly began. And then, she stopped herself, took a deep breath, and started again. "I'm trying my best, Ty!" she announced. In the front row, Nadia nervously straightened her headband.

"As you can see," Ms. Candy said, striking a pose, "I can't wait for tomorrow's Valentine's Day Celebration!" Jenny smiled. She had never seen her always-happy teacher happier. Ms. Candy was dressed in red high heels and black pants. Hearts of every color covered her sweater and the words "LOVE IS IN THE AIR!" were splashed across the front. Jenny wondered just how Ms. Candy would manage to top today's love-themed outfit at tomorrow's Valentine's Day Celebration. She thought about what ensemble Ms. Candy would wear for the actual Valentine's Day, which Jenny hoped that she would celebrate with Mr. Short.

"Don't forget to finish your cards!" With a wink she added, "I've already been given my first one!" A few of the boys made kissing noises, but Ms. Candy didn't seem to notice. As she salsa danced over to her desk, she sang, "Love is in the air!" And then in plain view of the class, Ms. Candy took a huge bite of a red velvet cupcake.

"Now, if the spelling bee and the Valentine's Day Celebration got you all riled up, then I know y'all must be really excited for the Fifth-Grade Soccer Game!" Ms. Candy said. Over the loud cheers, she shouted, "So, what do y'all think, are we gonna win?" The class exploded into shouts, high fives and fists pumps, and Jenny felt herself being swept up in a flood of happiness. "So, what are we waiting for?" Ms. Candy asked. "Time for soccer practice!" All at once, the class jumped up from their desks and hurried out of the classroom except Nadia, who reminded Ms. Candy that she needed to go to the nurse's office to take her allergy medication.

Jenny began to worry because she knew that Nadia was not really going to the nurse's office. Instead, she would probably write on the school supplies, the walls, maybe even the desks or the chairs—something—again. Hidden in the hallway, Jenny waited for her class to turn the corner toward the door that led out to the field. When she peered into the classroom, Nadia was already pulling out the black markers from inside her desk.

Jenny ran as fast as she could to catch up with her class, who were by now, halfway across the parking lot. Jenny quickly tried to think of a way to get someone, anyone, to go back into the classroom and discover what Nadia was up to. When the spy book's list of ideas to fake getting sick popped into her head, Jenny knew what she needed to do. Imitating one of Tyler's tricky soccer moves— the one where he crossed the ball under his left leg using his right foot—at full speed, Jenny kicked the air as hard as she could. This caused her to trip herself and fly onto the pavement.

"Owwww!" Jenny yelled out in pain and less than a minute later, her class had all run back to help her.

"Jenny!" Ms. Candy yelled. "Are you okay?" Jenny saw that her knee had begun to bleed and she shook her head. Ms. Candy examined the scrape and said, "It's not too bad, thank heavens, but I need a volunteer to go back into the classroom to fetch me a few Band-Aids."

"I'll go," Aidan offered right away, smiling down at Jenny. Walking back toward the school he joked, "I'm sure you guys won't miss me on the sidelines."

As she helped Jenny up, Ms. Candy shouted, "Get a wiggle on, Aidan!" and Aidan ran the fastest that anyone in the class had ever seen him move. Jenny's plan was working and she tried her best not to smile.

When Aidan walked into the classroom a few minutes later, the first thing he did wasn't shout or yell or even head straight to

Principal Brimstone's office to report what Nadia had done. Sighing, Aidan said, "It takes one to know one." Nadia looked up at him in shock, her headband hanging halfway off, her clothes soaked wet. Covering her face with marker-stained hands, Nadia began to cry. She had written "AIDAN" all over the classroom walls.

Ignoring both Nadia and the writing, Aidan headed toward the supply closet while Nadia desperately tried to clean the marker off the wall with a sponge and a bucket of soapy water. As he pulled out the Band-Aid box, Aidan turned toward Nadia and said, "That black marker is never going to come off, no matter how much soap you use."

Nadia stopped scrubbing. With wet hair hanging across her eyes, she glared at Aidan and asked, "How would you know?"

"Let's just say, I've had to clean up a lot of messes," he laughed. Aidan shoved the Band-Aids into his pocket and standing on his tiptoes, he reached into the back of the supply closet.

"What are you doing?" Nadia asked sharply.

Continuing to ignore her, Aidan reached his hand in even further. "Aha!" he cried, pulling out a key. Aidan walked over to the cabinet under the sink and slotted the key into the lock.

"We're not supposed to go in there!" Nadia screamed.

Aidan looked up at her calmly but sternly and asked, "Do you want to get the marker off or not?"

Nadia nodded her head and admitted, "Yes."

From the cabinet, Aidan pulled out two rags and a box of baking soda. "We need toothpaste!" he yelled.

"Toothpaste? Stop fooling around, Aidan! The class is going to be back soon!" Aidan shot Nadia a look that meant business. "Okay, okay," Nadia said. "I brush my teeth every day after we eat lunch."

"Figures," sighed Aidan. Nadia ran to her cubby and grabbed the toothpaste out of her backpack. She handed it to Aidan. "Thanks,"

Aidan said. From the recycling bin, Aidan pulled out an empty yogurt container and squirted in the entire tube of toothpaste. Next, he poured in the box of baking soda. Looking around the classroom, Aidan asked, "Spoon?"

Nadia hurried back to her cubby and rummaged through her lunchbox. "Aha!" she cheered and ran back to Aidan with a spoon. Nadia watched intently as Aidan began to mix the toothpaste and baking soda together. When he was finished, she said, "How do you know it will work?"

"I stink at math and spelling, but I'm really good at science," he said as the mixture turned into a gluey paste. "How could you forget last week's exploding volcano?" Aidan asked as he dipped one of the rags into the mixture. "And my step-mom, she's really good at crafts and homemade stuff." He began to rub the rag on an "AIDAN" and Nadia watched in disbelief as the black marker disappeared from the wall within seconds.

"Wow!" Nadia exclaimed.

"She taught me how to make this wall cleaner from scratch," Aidan bragged. "Works like a charm!"

For the next ten minutes, Aidan and Nadia toiled in silence, rubbing the writing off the wall. When they were almost done, Nadia looked up at Aidan and asked, "Why are you helping me after I tried to blame you?"

"Lately, you've been meaner to me than usual, so I know something's wrong," Aidan laughed. Nadia began to scrub the wall harshly. "Then all your new clothes," he continued. "And, the writing."

"I'm sorry, Aidan!" cried Nadia as she started to tear up. "My parents... they... they're getting divorced!" Nadia covered her face with her hands and sobbed.

"I know what you're going through," Aidan said. "My parents got divorced when we were in first grade."

Taken by surprise, Nadia looked up and asked, "They did?"

Aidan said, "I was mad and scared and I wanted a lot of attention, too. Why do you think I get in trouble?" For the first time since Aidan and Nadia could remember, they understood each other.

As she dipped her rag into the cleaning solution, Nadia said, "Remember when we were friends in kindergarten?"

Aidan nodded and said, "Remember when we used to play together every day at recess?"

Smoothing her wet clothes, Nadia said, "Back when I wasn't afraid to get dirty at recess."

Sighing, Aidan admitted, "Back when recess didn't make me so tired." Aidan checked the classroom for more black writing. When he found the last "AIDAN," he looked Nadia in the eye and said, "Promise you won't write on the walls or school supplies anymore?"

"Promise," Nadia agreed. And then, she picked up the black markers and threw them into the trash can.

"Nice shot!" cheered Aidan.

Nadia smiled and said, "Promise you'll stop all the silly pranks?"

"Promise," Aidan agreed. And then he pulled a deflated whoopee cushion out of his pocket and threw it into the trash can. "Anyway, this would have just made Tyler want to hate me even more."

"Bad attention is still attention," said Nadia.

"I know what you mean," laughed Aidan.

Aidan scrubbed the last "AIDAN" off the wall. "A-I-D-A-N," he read. Then he stared at Nadia and said, "N-A-D-I-A." Aidan put down his rag and said, "Huh. I never realized that we kind of share the same name."

Nadia emptied the soapy water into the sink and said, "I never realized that we kind of share the same problem."

As they were putting back the supplies, Aidan said, "You know what I also never realized, Nadia? You're actually not so good."

"You know what I also never realized, Aidan?" Nadia said, as she shut the supply closet door. "You're actually not so bad."

"Appearances can be deceiving," they said in unison, imitating Ms. Candy.

When they stopped giggling, Aidan looked at Nadia and smiled warmly. "The divorce? You'll be fine, trust me," he assured her, gently patting her shoulder. "Come on. Let's go back outside," Aidan said. "I've got to deliver these Band-Aids." Together, they ran out of the classroom.

Although she wasn't aware of all the details, when Aidan and Nadia ran onto the field together full of smiles, Jenny instantly knew that her plan had worked. Aidan and Nadia helped Jenny apply the Band-Aids to her knee, and all three of them sat on the sidelines cheering on their classmates. Ms. Candy asked, "How's the scrape, sugar?" and Jenny was reminded of her plan to help Ms. Candy and Mr. Short get together. Looking down at her knee, Jenny noticed the rows of Band-Aids and thought of rows of Chinese crullers, her mother's signature sweet. This gave her an idea about how she was going to help Mr. Short figure out that Ms. Candy felt the same way as he did.

As soon as they pulled into the garage after school, Jenny ran inside, threw down her backpack, washed her hands and began pulling out baking supplies from the cabinets and food pantry. When her mother walked into the kitchen, the counter was already covered with a bowl and a frying pan, plus a cup of water, salt, flour, and oil.

"I'm making Chinese crullers for school, Mommy!" Jenny announced.

Jenny's mother hung up her car keys and walked toward the food pantry. She pulled out the baking powder and baking soda, and placed them on the counter with the other supplies. "We need ammonia," Jenny's mother said.

"Ammonia?" Jenny challenged her. Her mother shot her a look that meant business. "Okay, okay, Mommy," Jenny said and she ran to the cabinet under the sink and pulled out the bottle of ammonia.

When she tried to hand it over, Jenny's mother laughed. She said, "That's for cleaning kitchen." She pointed to the food pantry and said, "ammonium bicarbonate" in Chinese. When Jenny handed her the ammonium, her mother said, "Yes. For baking," which caused them both to laugh this time.

Jenny's mother poured everything together into the bowl. Looking around the kitchen, she asked, "Chopsticks?" In the drawer, Jenny found two wooden chopsticks. Her mother smiled and handed one chopstick back. "One for you. One for me," she said, smiling.

Jenny and her mother stirred and kneaded the dough. While they waited for the dough to rise, they shared two pots of tea. And when the dough was ready, they rolled it, stretched it, sliced it and deep fried it in oil. Three hours later, as they placed the crullers into a box to bring to school, Jenny longed to ask her mother why she was helping her after all the scheming and scamming. But, Jenny thought better of it. She was finally out of her room and finally doing something fun together with her mom. Besides, Jenny already knew the answer—love—the kind that isn't just reserved for Valentine's Day.

Friday, February 12:
The New Queen Bee

Mixed in with Jenny's valentines was the red box containing two dozen Chinese crullers. As she and her mother were baking yesterday, Jenny had explained that each classmate would be given a card and a cruller, her mother's signature sweet, during the Valentine's Day Celebration. Jenny's real plan, however, was to pretend that the crullers were Ms. Candy's Valentine's Day present for Mr. Short. Jenny hoped that her mother wouldn't mind the change. Baking the crullers had brought Jenny and her mother together. Jenny hoped the gift would produce the same result for Ms. Candy and Mr. Short.

On the car ride to school, Jenny worried that she would have trouble sneaking the box into Mr. Short's classroom. As soon as Jenny arrived, however, and observed the pandemonium of a Friday jam-packed with grade-level bees and class Valentine's Day celebrations, she knew the task would be easy. Most of the class was running around and talking so excitedly that Jenny wondered if they had eaten their Valentine's Day candy for breakfast. Plus, Mr. Short's usually orderly room was cluttered with lots and lots of stuff: hundreds of decorated valentine's cards, valentine collection boxes for each student, Valentine's Day decorations and a table full of brightly colored cookies, cakes and candy. And best of all, Mr. Short was nowhere to be seen. Jenny was able to place the box of crullers on his desk and walk back out the door to her own classroom without anyone noticing.

Ms. Candy's classroom showed similar signs of craziness, and with her secret present safely delivered to Mr. Short, Jenny began to relax the second she stepped inside. "Simmer down, y'all!" Ms. Candy pleaded with the class. But, no one was listening. Just like Mr. Short's students, everyone was darting around the classroom, chattering energetically. Ms. Candy walked toward Jenny's desk in the middle of the classroom and tried again. "Y'all!" she shouted and when no one listened, she placed her hand on her hip in frustration. Jenny looked up at her teacher and smiled. Ms. Candy had indeed been able to top yesterday's love-themed outfit. With her knee-high black boots, she had paired a white silk dress covered with red hearts and a red belt with the word "LOVE." On her red sweater, she had fastened a pin that said, "Love a Southern Girl." Blonde ringlet curls peeked out from under a sparkly red sequined beret and her lips were painted with cherry red lipstick. Jenny didn't know anyone with more flair.

Ms. Candy reached into the pocket of her sweater. As she pulled out her whistle, she winked at Jenny and said, "This should get their attention!" Covering her ears, Jenny smiled. "FWEEEEEEEEEEE!" Immediately, everyone stopped what they were doing. "I know y'all are excited for today's activities," said Ms. Candy.

"Cookies!" yelled Jack.

"Cake!" yelled Aidan.

"Candy!" yelled Nadia, smiling as she looked back at Aidan, who gave her a thumbs up.

"Yes, we'll have lots of sweet treats at the Valentine's Day Celebration after lunch," said Ms. Candy. "But now, it's time for the Fifth-Grade Spelling Bee. Let's not keep Principal Brimstone or your parents waitin' any longer." Ms. Candy blew her whistle again as she high-stepped toward the front of the classroom. The class lined up behind Ms. Candy and enthusiastically marched out the door toward the auditorium.

Mr. Short had begun to line up his class for the spelling bee, too, when the red box caught his attention. Mr. Short walked over to his desk and read the note on top. It said, "TO: MR. SHORT. FROM: MS. CANDY." Immediately, he began to open the box. Mr. Short glanced at the clock. In two minutes, his class was supposed to be in the auditorium. When he picked up a cruller to take a bite, Mr. Short noticed that there were typed letters underneath. Quickly moving the crullers to the side of the box, Mr. Short was then able to read what turned out not to be letters, but a poem.

> You are Mr. Short.
> You are SWEET.
> Hope you like
> This special TREAT!

Adjusting his glasses as he finished not just one bite, but the entire cruller, Mr. Short read the poem again. Only when he heard Ms. Candy's whistle from the hallway did Mr.

Short's attention return to the classroom. He closed the box and led his class to the auditorium, whistling all the way.

"Good morning!" announced Principal Brimstone to the students, teachers and the audience of parents. "We're pleased as pie that you could join us for Haverswell Elementary's Fifth-Grade Spelling Bee. I'm sure y'all will have a swell time today!" After some polite laughter, Principal Brimstone repeated, "HAVERSWELL. HAVE. A. SWELL." Some of the kids began to hoot and holler, and Principal Brimstone said, "Anyway, it seems like everyone's anxious to get started, so without further ado, I will hand it over to our judge, the lovely Ms. Candy."

For the next hour, the fifth graders tried their hardest to stay in the competition by spelling words correctly when it was their turn. Jenny and Aidan got out in the first round, mostly because of nervousness. Jack made it to the third round but got out when he forgot to ask for a definition, spelling "way" instead of "weigh." Tyler and Tanner both got tripped up in the sixth round. Tyler forgot the "g" in "reign." Tanner spelled "discrepancy" with "ency" instead of "ancy." By the ninth round, the contest was narrowed down to two spellers—Nadia and Lilly. By the thirteenth round, they were still going at it. To start the round, Ms. Candy asked Nadia to spell "mischief."

"M-I-S-C-H-E-I-F," said Nadia quickly.

"Ooooh. I'm sorry, Nadia," said Ms. Candy. "That's incorrect." Accepting the bad news gracefully, Nadia nodded her head and then sat down in her chair. "Your try, Lilly," Ms. Candy said.

Lilly ran up to the podium, full of smiles. "I know this one!" she announced, which caused some commotion in the audience.

"Mischief," said Ms. Candy clearly. "Mischief."

"Mischief," Lilly said. "M-I-S-C-H-I-E-F."

Lilly held her breath until Ms. Candy announced, "That is correct." When Lilly began doing a victory dance across the stage, Ms.

Candy tapped the microphone to get her attention. "Hold on there, sugar. You've got to spell one more word."

"Oh. I thought I, like—" Lilly began. And then she stopped herself, took a deep breath, and started again. "I thought I had it." Lilly walked over to the microphone and brushing back her hair, she said calmly, "Ready, Ms. Candy."

Ms. Candy looked down at the next word and chuckled. "I'm sorry," she said. "But, this is ironic." She looked at Lilly and smiled. "Persevere," Ms. Candy said, "Persevere."

"Persevere," Lilly repeated. "P-E-R—" Lilly stopped for a moment. And then, using her finger to spell out the word in the air, just like she had done so many times in the past week with the marker on the dry erase board, Lilly started again. "P-E-R-S-E-V-E-R-E."

Lilly held her breath until Ms. Candy said, "Ladies and gentlemen, boys and girls, we have ourselves a winner!"

Lilly jumped into the air with as much enthusiasm as if she had scored a goal. "I did it!" she cheered. "I won! I won!"

Ms. Candy leaned toward the microphone and tried her best to speak over the applause. "Lilly has won movie tickets and will get to compete in next week's school-wide competition for a spot in the South Carolina State Spelling Bee." The noise in the auditorium was too overpowering, so Ms. Candy turned off the microphone and made her way across the stage to where Lilly was doing an extended victory dance.

When she noticed Ms. Candy, Lilly smiled deeply at her teacher and said, "Who would have guessed that I'd love spelling almost as much as soccer?"

"And, that you'd be so good at it!" Ms. Candy said. "All it took was practice!"

Lilly rolled her eyes and admitted, "And practice and practice and more practice."

"My little baby lamb," Ms. Candy said, wrapping her arms around Lilly. "I'm so proud of you!"

Lilly's parents stepped onto the stage. Her younger sister toddled right behind them.

"Great job, champ!" said Lilly's dad.

"Impressive," Lilly's mom said.

"Peer! Peer!" cheered Lilly's sister, and everyone laughed and clapped along with her.

Lilly's mom picked up her sister and she said, "Persevere."

Lilly kissed her sister's nose and said, "It means to win."

"It means more than just winning," said Ms. Candy. "It means that Lilly has overcome her problem with saying 'like' in a major way." Lilly's parents nodded in agreement.

"So, no speech evaluation?" Lilly asked her parents tentatively.

"No speech evaluation!" answered her parents.

Lilly quickly hugged her mom and dad, and gave her sister another kiss. Then she raced toward the other side of the auditorium. When she found Tyler, Lilly gave him such a powerful high-five that he was almost knocked down. "I can play in the soccer game!" she shouted, clearly and without any hint of a verbal pause.

On the other side of the stage, Nadia's parents had joined her, too.

"Sorry that you didn't win," Nadia's father said glumly.

"You're so negative," Nadia's mother said sharply. "Couldn't you have at least said, 'Good job!'?" Nadia stood quietly listening to her parents argue until she spotted Aidan in the audience gesturing her over.

"Mom? Dad?" Nadia asked. When her parents stopped talking she said, "I've got to go. My friend is waiting." With a quick wave goodbye, Nadia sprinted off the stage toward Aidan.

When she found him, Aidan shrugged his shoulders and said, "There's more to life than winning spelling bees."

Nadia looked up at him, thankful for the comforting words and happy that someone understood. She laughed and said, "Like cookies!"

Aidan cheered, "Like cake!"

"Like candy!" Nadia giggled.

"Exactly," said Aidan and together they walked out of the auditorium.

Boxes and boxes of pizza officially kicked off the Valentine's Day Celebration back in the classroom. When it was Jenny's turn to be served, she started to worry. She half-expected Ms. Candy to give her a piece of Aidan's birthday treat, the disgusting pizza cookie cake, and she was also nervous to try the real thing—she had never eaten pizza in her life. But because Jenny wanted to be like the rest of her class, and also because the hot pizza smelled really delicious, when Ms. Candy asked how many slices she wanted, Jenny answered, "Three, please."

After lunch, the room was once again filled with activity as the class delivered their valentines to the collection boxes. "No peeking!"

Ms. Candy joked. When the last valentine had been matched up to its intended recipient, Ms. Candy said, "Okay, y'all, you may open your valentines!" Looking just like her students, Ms. Candy ran over to her collection box, giddy with anticipation. "Hot dog!" she shouted.

For the next half an hour, the noises in the room ping ponged back and forth between "Cool!" and "How sweet!" plus the silence that accompanies both embarrassment and heartfelt appreciation. Although Jenny didn't say a word, her body felt all the same things. Two emotions Jenny also felt were surprise—all her classmates did indeed know her name—and something she could only describe to herself as warmth.

The valentine decorated in puce-colored tissue paper was Jenny's favorite. While many of Jenny's other cards were nice, the person who had made the puce card was the only one who had remembered her favorite color. At first, Jenny thought that Ms. Candy might have made the valentine, but then she opened it up and found a poem inside.

Jenny Lou.
Sweet, Jenny Lou.
If you only knew,
How much I like you.

Jenny couldn't help blushing, especially when she saw the three words that were written on the bottom of the card, "IT'S ALL GOOD." Immediately, Jenny began looking around for the Secret Note Writer. Aidan was sitting with Nadia in the back row, and when she caught his attention, he waved. Jenny smiled back, still unsure if it was him.

Then Aidan held up a valentine from Nadia's pile, which was in the shape of a pizza slice. Pointing at it, he smiled proudly as he mouthed, "The pizza's from me!" Jenny looked down at her pile and found an identical pizza-shaped card. It read, "I LOVE YOU MORE THAN PIZZA!" At that moment, with absolute certainty, Jenny knew that Aidan was most definitely not the Secret Note Writer.

Then, Jenny heard a tap on her desk and looked up. Ms. Candy was holding the valentine that Jenny had made for her. The card was decorated just like Ms. Candy had described her Miss South Carolina pageant dress, five layers of puce-colored chiffon ruffles sprinkled with stick-on diamonds.

"This is so special, Jenny," Ms. Candy whispered. "Just like you." Then, handing Jenny the second of her puce-colored valentines, Ms. Candy repeated what she had said on her first day at Haverswell Elementary, "We're so happy that you're here, Jenny!" When Ms. Candy wrapped her arms around her, this time Jenny knew exactly how to hug her back.

After Ms. Candy walked away, Jenny heard another tap on her desk, and when she looked up, Tanner was holding the valentine that Jenny had made him. She had decorated it with silver metallic paper to match his all-braces smile. "Cool paper," Tanner said softly as he tossed his bangs to the side. "No one else but you managed to get my favorite color right." Jenny blushed, flattered by the compliment but also wondering how Tanner knew the card was from her. She never got the chance to ask him because Ms. Candy announced that it was time for dessert, which sent everyone, including Tanner, rushing toward the tables at the front of the classroom.

Jenny had never seen so many neon-colored desserts: red velvet whoopee pie hearts, pink chocolate chip cookies, brownies with purple and white M&Ms, peanut butter cookies with Hershey Kisses stuck on top, lollipops, cupcakes, candy hearts and chocolate-covered strawberries, the healthiest of the bunch. For a whole minute, Jenny stood holding her empty Valentine-themed plate, staring at the dessert table. Used to smaller and less-brightly colored sweets, Jenny was partly disgusted and partly intrigued.

"Jenny," said Lilly, jolting her back to reality, "What are you going to try?"

"Everything," Jenny answered and then began loading up her plate.

When Jenny walked back toward her desk, Aidan motioned for her to sit with him and Nadia. "Man, that's a lot of food," Aidan said, "even for me." Jenny just smiled and then ate her way through the plate of desserts. When Ms. Candy gathered everyone on the carpet to read Valentine's Day poems, Jenny's horrible stomachache began. She felt even worse when Mr. Short walked over to Ms. Candy, with the box of crullers in his hands.

"I love the crullers!" exclaimed Mr. Short.

Ms. Candy seemed confused but said, "I love crullers, too!" Jenny should have been happy that her plan to get the teachers together was working, but her stomach was hurting too much to notice.

"What a SWEET TREAT!" continued Mr. Short. "I do love SWEETS!"

Ms. Candy laughed, "Me, too!"

Then Mr. Short put down the box of crullers. From behind his back, he pulled out a heart-shaped chocolate lollipop. Shyly, he handed it to Ms. Candy, who gushed, "Oh, my word! Another valentine, Mr. Short?" Mr.

Short looked confused, but smiled anyway as Ms. Candy said, "You shouldn't have!" Jenny's stomach throbbed with pain, but she didn't want to interrupt the moment between the teachers, so she held onto it tightly, attempting to hide the loud rumbles.

From his back pocket, Mr. Short pulled out a matching chocolate lollipop. "I never realized that you loved sweets, too!" exclaimed Ms. Candy.

"Appearances can be deceiving," he said, shrugging. And then Mr. Short tried to imitate one of Ms. Candy's winks, which caused his glasses to slide down his nose and made both teachers burst into laughter.

By the time she arrived at the piano studio for her lesson with Mrs. Sheldon, Jenny was buckling in pain from all the pizza and sweets. Although she was able to make it through the opening movement, when she got halfway through the middle of the piece, Jenny began to demonstrate all the symptoms that she had tried so hard to fake over the last week—chills, a fever, sweating and dizziness. She was certain that her face had turned a real shade of "Swamp Green."

"You look a little queasy," said Mrs. Sheldon. Jenny stopped playing and clutched her stomach. She could barely see straight. "Well, I guess it's natural for the star of the show to be a little nervous!" Mrs. Sheldon laughed. She wanted to be sick, but Jenny smiled as best as she could. Then Mrs. Sheldon looked up at the clock and said, "Go home and get some rest. I'll see you on Sunday at the recital!" Quickly, Jenny gathered her sheet music and stumbled outside to get some fresh air until her mother picked her up.

At home, Jenny changed into her pajamas, crawled into bed and tried to sleep. But, she couldn't. The stomach pains were making her toss and turn. She was also terrified about being the star of the piano recital, which was in two days. When Jenny's mother came to check on her, Jenny moaned, "Mommy, I need to practice."

"Rest," said Jenny's mother.

"But, the recital—" Jenny argued, starting to get up from bed.

"Big game tomorrow," Jenny's mother said, pulling the covers back over her. "Rest."

The last thing Jenny remembered before falling fast asleep was her mother's soft hand smoothing her hair while she sang her favorite Chinese lullaby.

SATURDAY, FEBRUARY 13:
THE GAME OF LOVE

The overpowering smell of ginger root stirred Jenny awake. Turning over in her bed, Jenny's stomach still felt a little sore from eating too much junk food at yesterday's Valentine's Day Celebration, but the fever and chills, and the sweating and the dizziness had disappeared. When she checked the time, Jenny could hardly believe her eyes. The alarm clock read, "11:48 AM," which meant that she had been asleep for almost nineteen hours straight. As she lay in bed deciding that she would never eat so much pizza or anything so fluorescent-colored ever again, Jenny finished the entire pitcher of water that her mother had left on her nightstand.

After she slowly stepped out of bed, Jenny stretched her hands toward the ceiling and then twisted side to side like she had seen Lilly and Tyler do to loosen up before soccer practice. In the bathroom, Jenny brushed her teeth four times before she took a shower. The hot water felt good on her skin. The lavender soap helped Jenny to feel both relaxed and refreshed, and also satisfied that any symptoms from yesterday's illness had been washed down the drain.

When Jenny walked into the kitchen dressed in her sports clothes, her mother was draining a pan of boiled ginger root in the sink. "Good morning," Jenny's mother said.

"Good morning, Mommy," Jenny answered. Jenny started to ask about her father, but then she remembered that he was travelling over the weekend.

Jenny's mother pulled out a chair from the table and motioned for Jenny to sit down. "I make tea," she said, turning toward the food pantry and pulling out her tea collection. "Dandelion or peppermint?" she asked Jenny.

Peppermint reminded Jenny too much of all the candy that had upset her stomach, so she said, "Dandelion, Mommy."

While she waited for the dandelion flower tea to brew, Jenny's mother mixed together lemon juice, water and salt in a bowl. Then, she placed the ginger pieces on a baking sheet and drizzled on the mixture. Seeing the sugar that her mother sprinkled on top made Jenny queasy, but she knew that ginger, which was good for calming down a stomach, would be way too bitter without it.

When she was finished, Jenny's mother placed the baking sheet in the oven and checked on the tea. She poured a cup for Jenny and brought it over to the table and said, "Sip." With each mouthful of tea, Jenny noticed herself feeling a little bit better. When the cup was finished, Jenny's mother brought it to the sink, then opened the oven, pulled out the baking tray and set it on a trivet on the counter.

As the candied ginger slices cooled, Jenny's mother found a hairbrush in her purse and began braiding Jenny's long hair. Jenny closed her eyes and breathed in the ginger and the dandelion smells, and thought about everything that had happened since she had arrived at Haverswell Elementary School. The last two weeks had been a mix of good news and bad news, but through all the chaos, Jenny had secretly managed to solve each of the three situations at school. "I did it!" she wanted to yell, just like Lilly did when she won the spelling bee.

Not only had Lilly learned to speak without saying "like" through Jenny's "Sounds Like Game," but her spelling bee win had convinced Lilly's parents that she didn't need a speech evaluation. This meant that Lilly would be playing in today's Fifth-Grade Soccer Game alongside her best friend and teammate, Tyler, and that Ms. Candy's class would have a better chance of winning the whipped cream party prize.

Jenny had also figured out that Nadia, and not Aidan, was the person who was writing on the school supplies. Without getting Nadia suspended for her behavior or Aidan wrongly suspended just because he was the class prankster, Jenny had made sure that all the writing would stop. In the process, Jenny had helped Nadia and Aidan to restore their friendship.

And, through secret poems and desserts, Jenny had been able to convince Ms. Candy and Mr. Short to admit that that they both loved sweets and each other, all by Valentine's Day.

Only one problem remained, Jenny's own. The recital was tomorrow, but Jenny still hadn't learned the entire piano piece and she still hadn't told her teacher, Mrs. Sheldon, the truth about her piano skills. Jenny knew there wasn't much she could do about those things now, though, because the Fifth-Grade Soccer Game was starting in less than thirty minutes.

"Pretty," Jenny's mother said when she was finished braiding Jenny's hair.

"Thank you, Mommy," Jenny said, smiling.

"Time for big game," Jenny's mother said. Jenny's mother walked over to the cooled candied ginger slices and placed them in a small paper bag, which she then handed to Jenny. "Bring for stomach."

"Yes, Mommy," said Jenny.

"I start the car," her mother said, picking up the keys.

"Right behind you," said Jenny and she followed her out the door holding a water bottle and the bag of candied ginger slices.

When Jenny and her mother arrived at the field, both Mr. Short and Ms. Candy's classes were warming up. Jenny's mother took a seat in the stands with the other parents while Jenny ran onto the field, tentative at first because of her sore stomach, but picking up speed when she got closer to her classmates.

"Hi, Jenny!" announced Ms. Candy as Jenny ran past. "Ready to play?"

"Yes!" said Jenny enthusiastically as she joined Tyler and Lilly, who were leading the class in warm-up drills.

"Jenny!" yelled Lilly when she saw her. "Can you believe I won the spelling bee?" Lilly held her hand up for a high-five and when Jenny went to slap it, she missed. Lilly laughed and said, "Just make sure your passes are better than that high-five, and you'll do an awesome job today."

"Let's win this thing!" cheered Tyler. Jenny smiled and got in line.

After the warm-up, the music teacher, Ms. Ellison, led the fifth graders in singing the South Carolina song. Thankfully, everyone remembered the words, and sang loudly and with pride, even on the second verse.

Our state has rivers, lakes, an ocean.
It's got our true devotion.
Oh, South Carolina pride!

Our state has mountains, it has beaches.
It's got Foothills, juicy peaches.
Oh, South Carolina pride!

Oh, South Carolina. Oh, South Carolina.
Oh, South Carolina!
We'll love you 'till the day we die!

On the sidelines, many of the parents seemed emotional, especially those, who like Ms. Candy, had lived in South Carolina all their lives. When Jenny looked over at her mother, she was smiling warmly, even though Jenny knew that most of the words probably didn't make much sense. But, the song had a catchy tune, which after years and years of music lessons, Jenny knew counted for a lot.

The Fifth-Grade Soccer Game was divided into two thirty-minute halves. Just as Jenny had predicted, Lilly and Tyler were unstoppable—dribbling, passing and scoring goals as if their lives depended on Ms. Candy's class winning. Mr. Short's class looked the opposite, exhausted and ready to call it quits. By the end of the first half, Ms. Candy's class had scored seven goals and Mr. Short's class had scored zero.

Jenny was happy to sit on the sidelines with Aidan and Nadia, and cheer on her class. The bag of candied ginger slices was almost gone. It turned out that a lot of people had an upset stomach after overindulging on pizza and sweets at the Valentine's Day festivities, and Jenny was happy to share her mother's homemade remedy.

At the halftime break, each class gathered with their teacher and refreshed with water and orange slices. "Y'all are on fire!" Ms. Candy yelled, unable to hide her delight. "No mercy for Mr. Short's class today!"

The class cheered, all except Jack, who said, "I don't get it." Jenny was thankful that he had asked the question because she didn't understand what Ms. Candy meant either.

Before Ms. Candy could explain, Lilly chimed in. "Our team is so good that we're not giving Mr. Short's class any chance to score!"

"We're totally ruling this game," yelled Tyler as he high-fived Lilly.

And then, Aidan said, "We're kicking their butts!" and everyone laughed at his funny joke, even Ms. Candy, even Tyler and especially, Nadia.

"Aidan's right," said Tyler. "We're totally going to win this game. So how about we make it a shut-out?"

The class cheered again, all except Jack, who said, "I don't get it." And again, Jenny was thankful that he had asked the question because again, she didn't understand what Tyler meant either. She admired Jack. He had taught her that it was okay to admit not to understand something, even if it felt uncomfortable.

"A 'shut-out' means we don't let them score," said Lilly. After Tyler and Lilly's idea sunk in, the class erupted into cheers, excited about the second-half plan.

"Y'all, let's just think about this—" Ms. Candy began, but it was too late. The starting whistle had already blown and both classes flooded back onto the field.

In the second-half, Ms. Candy's team quickly scored three more goals, increasing their lead to ten, but Mr. Short's team remained scoreless. With five minutes left in the game, Ms. Candy walked over to Jenny's group on the sidelines and announced, "Okay, y'all. Time to go in."

"No way!" screamed Aidan.

"I'm staying right here," protested Nadia.

Aidan and Nadia looked over at Jenny for support. Through Jenny's attempts at faking sick, she had learned a few techniques that might help her avoid being sent into the game. Even though it didn't hurt anymore, Jenny clutched her stomach and moaned, "Ughhh."

But quickly, Ms. Candy dismissed all three of them and said, "Oh, it's just nerves." And when Aidan, Nadia and Jenny refused to budge, Ms. Candy glanced toward the stands and whispered, "Listen, your parents will be madder than pigs on stilts if they don't get to see you play." Ms. Candy's honesty brought

Aidan, Nadia and Jenny to their feet, and all three chuckled with each other at the image of angry pigs trying to balance on stilts. As they subbed out with their teammates, Ms. Candy yelled encouragingly, "Only five minutes left!"

When Aidan and Nadia replaced Tyler and Lilly, they exchanged high-fives. When Jenny stepped in as the new goalie, she heard one of the defenders shout, "It's all good!" When she turned around, the left defender, Jack, was giving her a thumbs-up and the right defender, Tanner, was flashing his all-braces smile. As the game started up again, Jenny looked at Jack and Tanner's backs as they guarded the goal. She knew for sure that one of the boys was the Secret Note Writer.

Nadia and Aidan were no replacement for Lilly and Tyler. Nadia barely moved when the ball came close to her. Aidan tried to keep up, but with every additional minute of playing time, he had to stop to catch his breath more frequently. With the switch, the game was more fairly balanced and Mr. Short's team was able to take more control of the ball. On a few occasions, Mr. Short's offense got the ball close to the goal, but the defense, Jack and Tanner, always managed to kick it back the other way before their strikers could take a shot.

By the last minute of the game, everyone assumed it was all over, and that Ms. Candy's class would win ten to zero. Many of the parents started to climb down from the stands to help the teachers set up for the whipped cream party. Players on both sides of the field stopped trying so hard.

In the last ten seconds, one of Mr. Short's students booted the ball in a last show of frustration. But, instead of going out of bounds like everyone had expected, the ball stayed in and proceeded to roll past Aidan and Nadia toward the goal. Jack was out of position in defense because he was already celebrating with one of his friends. So when one of Mr. Short's strikers came running down the field to get the ball, Tanner was left alone to protect the goal.

From the sidelines, Lilly and Tyler realized what was happening and began to chant, "Don't let him score! Don't let him score!" Tanner sprinted over to challenge Mr. Short's striker, but he was running too fast. The next thing everyone knew, Mr. Short's striker had kicked back his foot and blasted the ball toward the goal.

The next few seconds were a blur to Jenny. She heard Lilly and Tyler chant, "Don't let him score! Don't let him score!" and her mother yell, "Go, Jenny!" and Ms. Candy scream, "Oh, sugar!" Then, Jenny saw Tanner's usual poise turn into panic as the ball came flying toward her, his usual all-braces smile missing.

Remembering Coach Adkins' "slow as a herd of turtles" comment during practice, Jenny decided that she wouldn't hide in the goal, her shell, like a scared turtle. She had failed at a lot of things in her life, and especially during this last two weeks, but she couldn't let Mr. Short's team score. She couldn't let down her team.

With no idea what she was doing, Jenny leapt into a jumping-jack pose and tried to spread herself across the goal as widely as she could. When the ball made contact with Jenny's face, the wind was knocked out of her, but she managed to grab hold of the ball on the way down to the ground. Still holding the ball, Jenny landed on her wrist. The pain wasn't noticeable until Jenny heard the final whistle blow and she was sure that Ms. Candy's class had not only won the game, but had pulled off a shut-out.

Carrying Jenny high on their shoulders to the whipped cream party, Tyler and Lilly couldn't stop talking about how Jenny had saved the game. Although the pain in her wrist was getting worse, Jenny felt overjoyed to be part of the reason for her class' celebration.

Like the dessert table at the Valentine's Day Celebration, like a lot of things at Haverswell Elementary, the whipped cream party was so different than anything Jenny had ever experienced. Each person in Ms. Candy's class was given an entire bottle of whipped cream and when Ms. Candy blew her whistle, they could spray it wherever and on whomever they wanted to. Jenny tried to forget about the pain in her wrist. She couldn't wait to experience the craziest thing she had ever done in her life.

"FWEEEEEEEEEEEE!" Ms. Candy blew her whistle and immediately, whipped cream was flying everywhere and covering everyone.

Jenny managed to shoot a few squirts at Aidan and Lilly, but then she stopped and grabbed her wrist in pain. It was hurting too much to continue. "Here," Jenny said handing her whipped cream can to Aidan. "I have to go to the bathroom!"

"Now?" Aidan said.

"Spray Tyler for me!" Jenny said in her loudest voice and with a sly grin, Aidan ran toward him.

Nadia was the only one who noticed that Jenny was crying as she headed toward the bathroom. At first, Nadia thought about telling Ms. Candy or even Aidan, but then she decided it would be too hard to get their attention in the midst of the frenzied whipped cream party. So, she took off running behind Jenny.

Cradling her wrist in her opposite hand, Jenny tried to make it to the bathroom before anyone noticed, especially her mother, who was still watching the whipped cream party. Although her wrist hurt badly, Jenny guessed that it wasn't broken because she could still move it. This meant that she would have to play the piece—the difficult, impossible piece—that she still hadn't learned yet, at tomorrow's piano recital.

By the time she reached the bathroom, Jenny was crying hysterically. With her wrist now injured, Jenny knew that her hard work and extra practice would be for nothing. Her mind raced, thinking about all the time she had wasted practicing piano and trying scams. And her mind was not quiet, as Dr.

Ma wished, but screaming at her—loudly—that it was all too much.

Jenny pulled open the heavy bathroom door and stuck her hand in the space between it and the doorframe. She was annoyed at everything, and desperate enough to try one final way get out of the piano recital—not a scam, but a way that would really work.

Just as Jenny went to slam her fingers in the door, Nadia arrived and yelled, "Jenny! No!" and at the last second, Jenny pulled out her hand and stopped the door with her foot.

After spending the entire afternoon in the hospital, Jenny was finally back home in bed. Her broken toe had been placed in a cast. For the next three months she would have to walk around on crutches. Jenny and her mother were relieved that her wrist wasn't broken, as well, but only strained. When Jenny's mother walked into her bedroom, she brought a bag of ice to help soothe Jenny's swollen wrist.

"Thanks, Mommy," Jenny said.

Then, Jenny's mother pulled out Jenny's notebook from under the pillow and handed it to her. "I get pen," she said.

Shocked that her mother knew where she kept the secret notebook and at the fact that she was letting her have it, all Jenny managed to say was, "I can't write."

Jenny's mother placed the pen in Jenny's non-injured hand and she said, "Try your best. Writing good for you."

"Yes, Mommy," said Jenny and then her mother walked downstairs to prepare a pot of tea for them to share.

SUNDAY, FEBRUARY 14:
SPEAKING OF TRUTH

Haverswell Elementary School's auditorium
was already filling up with people when Jenny and her mother walked in. As they made
their way across the room—Jenny's crutches
hitting the wooden floor with a loud clunk
each time she took a slow, strenuous step—
Jenny was aware of only one thing, the piano
sat front and center of the stage. By the time
Jenny had woken up that morning, her mother had already called her piano teacher, Mrs.
Sheldon, and told her the bad news about
Jenny's broken toe and sprained wrist. When

Jenny found out about the call, she had begged her mother to go the Valentine's Day Recital, anyway, claiming that her wrist felt much better and that she was well enough to play.

In reality, Jenny's wrist was still sore. Plus, she still hadn't learned the entire piece. If she went to the recital, Jenny knew that she wouldn't be the "Star of the Show." Instead, with her mother, Mrs. Sheldon and the entire audience as witnesses, Jenny would be the "Joke of the Show"—her nightmare come true.

Jenny's injuries were the perfect excuse, the excuse she had been waiting for all along to get out of the recital. And, Jenny's mother had even been the one to decide that she wouldn't have to play. Maybe it was because Dr. Ma's special tea was starting to work. Or maybe it was because she had almost broken her fingers. Or maybe it was because her mother had said it was okay for her to do her best instead of being perfect. But, something inside of Jenny had changed. All of a sudden, her mind had quieted down.

In that silence, Jenny had found the solution to her own problem about the difficult piano piece. It was now clear to Jenny that all she needed to do, all she had ever needed to do, was to tell the truth. It might be embarrassing for Jenny to admit that her piano skills weren't as good as Mrs. Sheldon believed. She might play the piece terribly. But at least Jenny would be true to herself, true to who Jenny Liu really was.

Truth, Jenny decided, was exactly how she had helped Ms. Candy and Mr. Short, and Nadia and Lilly, solve their problems. And, that was what the Secret Note Writer was trying to tell her the whole time. It's all good. Who Jenny really was, turned out to be just right.

Step by step, Jenny climbed the stairs and then hobbled backstage, where Mrs. Sheldon was preparing her students for the show. "Oh, Jenny!" Mrs. Sheldon exclaimed when she saw her. "What are you doing here?"

Before Jenny could answer her mother said, "Jenny wants to play."

"But, her poor toe!" said Mrs. Sheldon. "Mrs. Liu, I really don't think you should make her perform."

"I want to play," said Jenny, smiling at her mother.

"Are you sure, Jenny?" asked Mrs. Sheldon.

"Yes," said Jenny. "I'm going to try my best." Jenny smiled as she rested her head on her mother's shoulder.

"Okay," agreed Mrs. Sheldon. "Let's get you warmed up, then."

"Wait!" Jenny said to Mrs. Sheldon, straightening up. "First, I need to tell you something."

Jenny's mother said, "I go," and she began to walk away.

"Wait!" Jenny said to her mother. "You, too, Mommy."

Jenny's mother stopped. She and Mrs. Sheldon looked at Jenny with anticipation. Jenny did not stare at the ground when she spoke. She took a deep breath and looking both of them straight in the eye, she admitted, "The piano piece is too hard for me. I learned the opening and most of the middle, but I need way more practice." The truth was finally out.

"Oh, Jenny," said Mrs. Sheldon. "I wish you had told me earlier! You were probably worried sick about the recital!"

Laughing to herself, Jenny thought, "If Mrs. Sheldon only knew!" The spy book and all Jenny's scams to make herself seem ill, seemed incredibly ridiculous now.

Jenny's mother took her hand. In Chinese she said, "Jenny, I want you to try your best. If you do that, you'll be fine." And, then Jenny's mother did something she hadn't done for a very long time. She leaned toward Jenny and hugged her so tightly that both mother and daughter could feel each other's hearts. "Trust me."

The warm feeling that Jenny experienced after she had opened her cards at the Valentine's Day Celebration came rushing back and she said, "I do, Mommy. I do." And, then Jenny turned to Mrs. Sheldon and said, "It won't sound very good, but I'm still going to play the difficult piece today. I made a promise and I don't want to let you down."

Turning toward Jenny's mother, Mrs. Sheldon said, "Mrs. Liu, why don't you take a seat in the audience. I have a solution that might work for everyone."

"It's okay, Mommy," Jenny said.

As Jenny's mother walked toward the stairs, she looked at Jenny and smiled. "Remember, try your best," she said.

When Jenny's mother was gone, Mrs. Sheldon said, "Do you think you will be ready to play the difficult piece by the Spring Recital? It's in May, about three months from now."

This time, Jenny answered her teacher honestly. "I'll have to practice really hard." Thinking of Lilly's winning spelling bee word Jenny added, "But I think I can persevere."

"Great!" said Mrs. Sheldon. "I like your attitude, Jenny!" Mrs. Sheldon walked over to her briefcase and began rifling through a book of piano music. When she found the page she was looking for, Mrs. Sheldon brought the book over to show Jenny.

"Would this be an okay piece for you to play today, especially with your sore wrist?" she asked.

Jenny looked at the music and realized that one of her piano teachers in California used to warm her up with the same piece at every weekly lesson. Jenny could play the music by heart. "Yes," she said.

"Great!" said Mrs. Sheldon and then she glanced down at Jenny's cast and said, "Now, what do we do about your foot?" Mrs. Sheldon thought for a moment and then said, "My grandson is in the audience today. He's a great little piano player. Why don't you go ahead and warm up and I'll see if he won't mind working the foot pedal for you."

An hour later, after all the other students had played, it was Jenny's turn. When Mrs. Sheldon went up to the microphone, Jenny stepped out from behind the curtains and using her crutches, she started to walk toward the piano. "I'm pleased to introduce our last performer," Mrs. Sheldon said. "Jenny Liu is our newest student and comes to our small town of Haverswell, South Carolina all the way from California." The audience responded with a handful of oohs and ahhs.

"And, this little lady really is The Star of the Show," Mrs. Sheldon continued, which caused Jenny to freeze in her tracks. "Jenny insisted on playing today, even though she sprained her wrist and broke her toe, just yesterday! Can you believe her dedication?" After the audience stopped applauding, Jenny smiled and started hobbling again. In a few steps, she made it to the piano bench and very carefully sat down.

As Jenny spread out her music, Mrs. Sheldon said, "Oh! The foot pedal! I almost forgot." And then, looking out into the audience, she yelled, "C'mon up, honey."

The stage lights made it difficult for Jenny to see exactly who was walking toward the stage. As Mrs. Sheldon's grandson made his way up the stairs, Jenny was able to see only one thing—a shiny all-braces smile—that a few seconds later, she discovered belonged to

Tanner. "Please give a round of applause to my grandson, Tanner," said Mrs. Sheldon. "He's helping out today." The audience applauded again. "Okay, you two," Mrs. Sheldon said. "Whenever you're ready!"

The pair sat together in silence for a few seconds until Tanner counted, "One, two, three." Then automatically, Jenny began to move her fingers across the keys. For the next five minutes, Jenny played the piece effortlessly, mostly from memory, as Tanner worked the foot pedal. When they finished, the audience roared with applause. Jenny's mother stood up and cheered the loudest of all.

Jenny smiled at Tanner and said, "Thanks."

"It's all good," Tanner said, flicking his bangs.

Jenny couldn't believe it—Tanner was the Secret Note Writer! As she started to say something back to him, Jenny heard someone yell out, "Jenny! Jenny!" Jenny turned and saw Ms. Candy and Mr. Short running toward her. For the second time in just a few moments, Jenny was speechless, truly speech-less. Ms. Candy was dressed in her Miss South Carolina pageant dress.

"I wore my favorite puce-colored dress just for you, Jenny!" Pointing at her dress, Ms. Candy asked, "She's a real beauty, isn't she?"

Before Jenny could answer, Mr. Short looked adoringly at Ms. Candy and said, "Yes, she is."

Ms. Candy giggled and said, "Oh, you're too sweet, Mr. Short!"

Then Ms. Candy hugged Jenny tightly and said, "Aren't you the bee's knees? You saved that goal yesterday and now you're up here playin' piano with your hand all wrapped up! What surprises do you have in store for us next, Jenny Liu?"

Jenny's mind filled with possibilities and at the same time, the stage began to fill with people, who Jenny slowly began to realize, were her classmates. Jenny was over-whelmed—they had all come to see her play! One by one, each classmate visited the piano bench to congratulate Jenny on the piano performance, wish her a Happy Valentine's Day and sign her cast.

Tyler and Lilly presented Jenny with the winning soccer ball from the Fifth-Grade Soccer Game. In addition to having everyone from Ms. Candy's class sign the ball, on the top they had written, "Jenny Saves the Game!"

"Epic job on the piano," Tyler said.

"Awesome," Lilly added as she high-fived Jenny's non-injured hand. This time, Jenny slapped her back.

"Thanks," said Jenny.

When Nadia walked over to Jenny she said, "I'm impressed!"

"Thanks for saving my fingers yesterday," said Jenny.

"Thanks for not telling on me about the writing," Nadia whispered. Jenny nodded.

Aidan bounded over to the piano bench and asked, "What did the elephant do when he hurt his toe?" When Jenny shook her head, Aidan cackled, "He called a toe truck!" Aidan was laughing so uncontrollably, he could barely speak. This time, Jenny understood the joke and she laughed right along. "I made you laugh!" Aidan beamed.

Jack looked confused and said "I don't get it." Then quickly, he added, "Never mind. Awesome job playing piano, Jenny!"

After all her classmates had said goodbye, Jenny and Tanner sat alone on the piano bench. Jenny thought about just how much Tanner's three words had helped her feel that everything in this new and very different place would somehow be okay.

"It's all good," Jenny said and Tanner nodded back.

"Happy Valentine's Day," Tanner said, smiling.

"Happy Valentine's Day," said Jenny.

And, truthfully, it was.

Jean Ramsden, a graduate of Cornell and Harvard, lives in North Carolina with her husband and four children.

31495712R00158

Made in the USA
Charleston, SC
19 July 2014